PRAISE FOR

# THE PLUNGE

## AN AGGIE MUNDEEN LAKE MYSTERY

"Deceit, disaster, and murder. A spellbinding episode in the life of this complex, likable heroine."
—*James W. Ziskin, Author of the Anthony and Macavity Award-winning Ellie Stone mystery series.*

"I was at the edge of my seat reading this fast-paced adventure."
—*Socrates Book Review*

"This was part mystery, part disaster and part second chances."
—*Carla Loves to Read*

"A frightening but heartwarming mystery…. I was surprised and gratified at the conclusions."
—*Mallory Heart*

"You will find yourself holding your breath as you read."
—*Laura Loves to Read*

# THE PLUNGE

## AN AGGIE MUNDEEN LAKE MYSTERY

## NANCY G. WEST

**WILDSIDE PRESS**

# ONE

## AGGIE MUNDEEN

### October 1998

"It's a shame somebody stole Chuck's boat," Sam said, his brown eyes focused on the road. A shock of brown hair flecked with gray drooped over his horn-rims. He was driving us to Lake Placid, one of a string of lakes on the Guadalupe River, thirty-five miles away from San Antonio Crime. He reached over to squeeze my hand. "I'm glad we have a whole weekend, Aggie."

I smiled. "Me, too."

"I've known Chuck Atwell a long time. This place is his getaway from the Houston hustle. He's on the executive fast track and can't get here very often. Nice of him to let us use the place." He looked over and raised an eyebrow above his glasses. "Let's investigate the theft quietly and not mention I'm a San Antonio Detective."

Without saying so, Sam was reminding me not to act on impulse. Obsessively curious and determined to right wrongs, I'd butted in more than once on a fascinating case. Sam was so work-oriented, how else could I get his attention? If my amateur sleuthing helped solve a crime, impressed him *and* buoyed my flagging self-esteem, so much the better.

It hadn't been all smooth sailing, though. After I created unintended fiascos and nearly got killed, he made it clear that if I stumbled on a crime and felt compelled to investigate, I better consult him. I could deal with that. He was worth it. I was ready for a crime-free weekend with the man I loved in a lakeside cottage on a slice of paradise. Maybe Sam could relax a little.

"Chuck said he found a shell soap dish missing, but it wasn't valuable."

That was Sam, always focused on crime. I sighed and rolled down the window. On both sides of Interstate Highway 10, smattering rains had greened the foliage. I let the wind hit my face. Like a bird released from a cage, I was over-flying the fields sliding past.

I hadn't helped Sam solve a case since last spring. Our Fiesta weekend on the River Walk turned into a frantic search for poor Monica's killer. Then my new friends' convention ended, and the girls all scattered. It wasn't my fault that when I spotted the killer, the girls ended up in the river.

After that, my life got pretty dull. I'd been ensconced in my Burr Road bungalow, bored to death. My next-door neighbor Grace, usually available for coffee and offering me sage counsel, was busy tiling table tops. Classes offered at local universities didn't intrigue me, and there were no other crimes I could help Sam solve, at least none I knew about. I even wondered if I should keep writing my Dear Aggie advice column. Maybe I needed a change.

When a couple of raindrops spattered my face, I rolled up the window. Sam peered up through the windshield. "Sky's kind of dark." He frowned. "Let's see what the weatherman says." He turned on the radio, and a voice blared.

*Weather patterns suggest a storm might develop.*

"That's vague." He flipped around the dial and landed on KWED, the radio station for Seguin, near Lake Placid.

*There's a potential for heavy rain Saturday night and Sunday.*

I shook my head. "That won't matter. We can sit under the patio and watch the rain." I wasn't about to let a little water derail our weekend. "How much farther is it?"

"We're almost there." A sign routed us off Interstate Highway 10 onto Highway 90A toward Seguin. Several yards down the road, a yellow light blinked in front of a brick façade: "Lake Placid Estates." The sign was a misnomer. There were no estates, only various-sized houses on both sides of a winding road. Houses on the left faced the lake. Homes on the right faced the road, the lake visible from front yards. The rain stopped, so I rolled down the window. I loved the smell of fresh water and caught glimpses of the lake through the trees. Ruffled by wind, the water was moving fast.

Sam pointed lakeside. "That's where Art Lively lives. He knows Chuck and invited us to tonight's homeowner's meeting."

"Sounds nice." As long as I was with Sam, I didn't care where we went. After two years of a contentious professional relationship, we had grown close in the past few months. We turned off Lake Placid Drive into Chuck Atwell's property, rolled up the circular drive and stopped at the low wrought iron gate.

I jumped out of his Chevy Caprice. "Lake first?" I asked, trying not to bounce with excitement.

"You bet." Sam grinned. We walked across an open-air brick patio toward the lake. In the center of the patio, a pecan tree five feet in diameter spread protective arms over a cottage on either side, wind gusts fluttering its leaves. The front of the patio overlooked the lake, under a roof connecting the two houses. Upriver and down, pecan, cypress, and elm trees rose from the bank, creating a waving canopy. The river undulated by, choppy rolls of water bumping fallen tree limbs downriver.

Sam pointed, "Look at the ducks." Geese, mallards, and wood ducks bobbed along, oblivious to the pulse of rising swells.

The lawn sloped thirty feet down to a U-shaped wood plank dock used to house Chuck's boat. The river side leg went around the far side of the missing boat. On the land side, the pathway extended across the front of the property. Sam pointed to a metal ladder bolted to the dock with rungs that led down to the river.

"The water looks higher than I remember. See the third step? You can usually see the whole thing. Now there's water lapping over it. If the water got high enough, it could have raised the boat so the tie ropes broke or came loose and the boat drifted out."

"I suppose." I wished he'd stop fretting and relax. As he walked down flagstone steps, I walked toward the car to unload but turned to watch him. He crouched on the dock by a metal stanchion, studied it and pulled at the attached rope. He walked around the dock to check the outside cleats. Sam swam better than I did, but watching him squat on the narrow walkway with the wind picking up, pulling on cleats to see if they were securely bolted, made me nervous.

He called to me. "The ropes didn't break, and they weren't cut. The thief untied them and slipped them off. He must not have been in a hurry." He stood, hands on his hips. "Anybody who drives a boat could have done this." His gaze moved from nearby homes to those across the churning river.

"I wonder who else besides Chuck has keys to the boat?" I said.

"I'll ask him." He paused. "Maybe we should pay some neighbors a visit."

He came up the steps. We would stay in the larger house with the kitchen. The small one was used as a guest house. Shadow boxes attached to its outside wall near the entry door displayed a collection of rocks and shells.

"Look, Sam, do you think previous guests gathered those as mementos?"

He nodded slowly, distracted by debris swirling down the river. "Could be."

He unlocked the door to the main house. We grabbed overnight bags from the back seat of the car and carried them inside. I helped him haul a cooler packed with food into the kitchen. The cottage was homey, with Saltillo tile floors, wicker chairs with cushions, and a few wrought iron tables. The roomy kitchen flanked with windows gave grand views of the lake. A bedroom and bath were at the back. I loved it. Maybe we could buy the cottages from Chuck and live there some day.

While Sam carried our bags to the bedroom, I unloaded the cooler, ran water over the fresh chicken we'd eat later and rubbed seasoning and olive oil into the skin. Even grocery chicken smelled fresher lakeside. Sam returned in cargo shorts, grinning. His shoulders looked relaxed, as though he was beginning to unwind.

He scanned the lake. "Beautiful view, huh?" He contemplated the neighbor's lawn to the left. "That's Alice Stapleton's house." Grass grew around a birdbath surrounded by dandelions and a tangle of weeds. Half-buried, barely recognizable objects dotted the lawn. "Chuck said she sees everything. She might be a good person to interview."

"Want me to come?" I dried my hands and headed toward the bedroom. "I'll be ready in five minutes."

Sam rubbed his chin. "He said she's a little eccentric. She might be more forthcoming if you talk to her alone."

Considering the weird accumulation of relics protruding through the grass, how did the house look inside? How would Chuck's neighbor view a stranger?

I took a deep breath. "Okay." I said. "I'll see what Alice knows about boat keys."

# TWO

I walked down our driveway studying Alice's lawn. Anchors—old, new, and rusted—nestled in the grass alongside decorative life preservers you might find at a nautical shop. Various-sized geese, ducks, and flamingos made of metal, wood, and plastic peeked above grass blades.

Sam hated disorder. No wonder he didn't want to come with me. I reminded myself not to tell Alice he was a detective, so he could discreetly investigate the theft of Chuck's boat.

I walked up Alice Stapleton's driveway past her vintage lime green Mercury. If her yard was a mess, what would the inside of her house look like?

She opened the door smiling. "Yes?" Bushy auburn hair poked from her head. She'd planted a stiff pink bow in the upper right quadrant. Her intense blue eyes sparkled with merriment. With her paisley shirt, bright green skirt, neon orange tennis shoes and white socks, she could be a leprechaun stationed in the yard, watching over her treasures.

"I'm Aggie Mundeen. Sam and I are staying at Chuck Atwell's house for the weekend."

"Ah. You must be a good friend of his. Chuck's a dear man. It's so nice to meet new neighbors, even temporary ones. Do come in."

The room was bright and cheerful. Dust particles floating in rays of sunlight highlighted so many artifacts, I could barely take them in. "You have quite the collection here."

She beamed. "I love garage sales. I buy whatever appeals to me. I have trouble letting go of anything." She giggled. "I suppose I'll have to build a bigger house one of these days."

Her delight made me smile.

"Sometimes," she said, "I get Verna Weller to go with me." She pointed at a house across the lake. "She and I compete for goodies. Her husband Maxwell doesn't like it one bit. He and I have shouting matches over it, but I don't pay him much attention. He's usually out fishing anyway. He just doesn't appreciate beautiful things."

"Some men don't." I moved through her collection, stopping for closer looks. I paused at a miniature wood duck and fingered the colorful feathers glued on. "This is lovely." A set of soap dishes shaped like sea shells in graduated sizes caught my eye. "This is a nice set. Is there a size missing?"

She nodded. "I gave it to Chuck when he admired it. Next thing I knew, I saw it in Verna's bathroom. I didn't ask how it got there."

Was that the soap dish Chuck said was missing? I picked up a bottle and peered through the glass at some sort of lake creature. I quickly put it down.

"I'm not sure what that is," she said. "Verna picked it up when we shopped together and decided later she didn't want it. Sometimes Verna calls people to see if they want to part with knickknacks. Makes Max furious when he finds out. He resents her spending money on trinkets when he could buy more fishing gear."

She put her hands on her hips and shook her head. "To think I once had my eye on him. We both lived on the lake, so I saw him a lot." She shrugged. "After Bob died—Verna's first husband—Max chased after Verna, moved her out to the lake and dumped me." She screwed up her impish face. "I still enjoy getting her to buy stuff so I can watch Max get mad. 'Course I lost everything in the '87 flood, just like Verna did. I've been doubling up on purchases lately. Buying goodies makes me feel secure, as if the weather knows better than to try to demolish my treasures. Silly isn't it?" She stroked the back of a china horse with a chipped tail.

"Not really. We all do things to comfort ourselves. Does the lake flood very often?"

"Every five to ten years or so. It depends how much it rains, how high the river gets, and how long it stays that way. And some houses sit higher than others. Ours are pretty high on this side of the lake."

"I'm glad about that. I can see you love your treasures."

"I knew I was going to like you, Aggie. Come over any-time." Having suffered losses, she seemed charmingly optimistic about the prospects of re-supply.

"I was so intrigued by your collection, I almost forgot. Chuck asked us to check his house because his boat was stolen. Did you see anybody fooling with the boat or walking around the property?"

"No. If I've had a good day at the sales, I sleep like a corpse. Somebody must have stolen it at night. I didn't hear a motor or anything. A few days ago, I realized the boat was gone and called Chuck."

"Do you know if anyone has a key to his boat?"

"Well, I don't. I probably couldn't back it out of the dock. He might have given a key to one of the men around here so if the water starts rising, they can get his boat out."

"I see. You might keep an eye out for anyone suspicious, just in case. Lock your doors."

"I doubt anybody would want anything in here." She giggled. "Before they got to the house, they'd probably trip over something."

"Are you going to the homeowners' meeting?"

"Not this time. Max and Verna will probably be there. She and I went to a sale yesterday, and I don't want to get into it with him."

"I'll see you again over the weekend?"

"Sounds good."

I smiled and walked out. For someone who didn't like Max, she sure talked about him a lot. Maybe his dumping her hurt more than she let on.

# THREE

When I walked across the patio, Sam was sprawled in one chair with his feet propped on another, and his head rolled back. He was snoring.

"Hey, Sam." I nudged his shoulder. "Sorry to wake you."

He rubbed his hands over his face and mumbled, "Ish okay. How did you and Alice get along?"

"Fine, actually." He moved his feet from the chair and I sat. "She loves garage sales. Trouble is, she never wants to throw anything away."

He laughed. "I gathered that from the lawn."

I winked at him. "And *I* gathered that's why you didn't want to go with me."

His smile faded. "Did she know anything about Chuck's boat?"

"No. She didn't hear anything or see anyone suspicious. She's a heavy sleeper. Thinks the thief probably stole it at night. She said Chuck may have given the boat key to a neighbor to get the boat out if the river rises."

"Okay. I'll call Chuck tomorrow. Let's meet our other neighbor, Garner Sledge. Give me five minutes to wash my face and wake up."

We walked past the guest cottage, across a wide expanse of grass to Garner Sledge's house. The closer we got, the larger it appeared. Built on stilts, two stories soared above the ground. His cars were parked under the house: a sleek black BMW and a Range Rover. Stairs led to the front door that overlooked the lake. Before we reached the landing, a man threw open the door, filling the door frame. From his height and girth, he must weigh over three hundred pounds.

"Hey," he bellowed. "I wondered when my low-dwelling neighbors were coming by."

"Low-dwellers?" Sam glanced at me. I shrugged. "I'm Sam Vanderhoven and this is Aggie Mundeen. We're house-sitting Chuck Atwell's place."

"Yeah, I know. I'm Garner Sledge. Come on in." He gestured toward Chuck's place. "When you're high up out of the flood plain, everybody at ground level looks like a low-dweller."

Sam nodded slowly. "I see. We're pretty comfortable over there."

"It's a nice house," Garner said with a shrug.

He moved inside. A massive portrait of Sledge in a Marine uniform hung behind him.

"Nice picture," Sam said, in exactly the same tone as Garner when he commented on Chuck's house. We strolled into the living room.

"Thanks. I'm pretty proud of my service," Garner bragged. "You ever serve?"

"No." Sam turned and looked steadily at Garner. "I got a deferment for law school."

"Law school, huh?" He snorted. "Too bad. You learn a lot in the Corps."

"I've learned plenty." To cut off further discussion of law school and his job as a police officer since then, Sam turned around to focus on a large wall picture of a polo match. "Are you a polo player?"

"Nope." Garner swept his arm around the room. "I just like to look at beautiful things."

Leather was everywhere—sofas, chairs, book bindings, leather holders for whiskey bottles, and mats around pictures of the polo match. Every item was large, solid and expensive. I was surprised Garner wasn't wearing a leather glove. A luxurious kitchen gleamed behind a copper bar trimmed with padded leather. This floor must be the leather museum and entertainment area, with sleeping quarters upstairs.

"Chuck asked us to come down and check his place because his boat was stolen. I thought you might have seen something from up here."

"I saw the empty dock after the boat was gone. I figured he was out fishing. He came over later and told me somebody stole it. Those executives buy classy boats. I guess somebody couldn't resist."

"Do you have any idea who took it?"

He shook his head. "Could be anybody on the river. A lot of people who don't live on the lake launch boats at the slip under the I-10 overpass." He jerked his thumb toward the road behind our houses. "Somebody could walk up from this road to the dock to undo the ropes."

"Do most people just tie their boats with simple knots, with no locks or anything?" I asked.

"Sure. Nobody messes with other people's boats unless there's a flood forecast, and we need to get somebody's boat out. Chuck gave me a key in case that happens. That's one reason I'm glad I don't have a boat."

"Chuck would probably let you use his to go fishing," Sam said.

"He probably would if I wanted to fish. Which I don't." He looked at his watch. "I'm a builder and realtor. I have to show a house." His eyes lit with pleasure. "These people really like to fish."

"You haven't seen anybody suspicious around Chuck's place?" Sam said.

"No, but I'm gone a lot. Pretty busy." He looked at his watch again.

"You didn't hear a motor start during the night?" I said.

"After a couple glasses of bourbon, I don't hear anything. That's why I installed an alarm. Y'all going to the homeowners' meeting?"

"Art Lively invited us to meet the neighbors."

"Great. We can talk there. It starts in a little over an hour." He waved us toward the front door, locked up, and plodded behind us down the steps. As we walked across the lawn, we heard the roar of his Range Rover.

"Did you notice there were no medals on Sledge's uniform?" Sam said.

"No. Do Marines always have medals?"

"They have at least one insignia."

"If anybody was going to display them, I think Garner Sledge would."

"Exactly."

"Do you think we have time for one more visit? After talking with Alice Stapleton, I'd like to meet Verna and Max Weller across the river. If we change for the meeting now, we can drive to the Wellers' and then back to Art's house."

"Sounds like a plan."

Sam changed into chinos while I dressed and freshened my makeup. I turned to him as I combed my hair. "Pour us some wine?"

"Sure." He brought me a glass and we clicked them together. "To us."

While I put on my earrings, Sam carried his glass to the wicker sofa and flipped on the TV, turning to the Weather Channel. The announcer's voice drifted into the bathroom.

*The remnants of hurricanes Lester and Madeline in the eastern Pacific are pushing a high level of moisture east across Texas. Thirty- to forty-knot winds flowing from the Gulf of Mexico are bringing low-level moisture from the southeast. The convergence may bring rain to Central Texas on Saturday and Sunday.*

Rain in Texas was always welcome. I finished my wine and put on lipstick. "Ready to see the other side of the river?" I asked as I walked into the living room.

Verna and Max lived across the lake in the Pecan Cove subdivision. Alice had pointed out their house, so I knew we could find it. We drove out of Lake Placid Estates, turned right on highway 90A and crossed the bridge over the lake. A block farther down, we turned right into Pecan Cove, on to Turtle Lane. Like Lake Placid Drive, Turtle Lane ran the length of the subdivision, made a U-turn at the end where cul-de-sac houses faced the water, and circled back to the entrance. About twelve houses down, I craned between houses and saw Chuck's cottages across the lake. The land and houses were much higher on the other side.

"Slow down, Sam. This must be the Wellers' house."

The two-story home sat on stilts like Garner Sledge's, but the stilts were taller. The home was considerably smaller. When we knocked, Verna Weller, blond and petite, opened the door.

"Sam and Aggie? I was hoping you'd come by," she said. "Alice called and said how nice you were." She smiled at us and offered Sam her hand.

"Yes, ma'am. I'm happy to meet you."

I loved it when his Southern manners showed.

She ushered us inside. The room reminded me of a doll house replicated to normal size. Every piece of furniture was perfectly spaced against a wall with a group of items on top and a painting hanging behind that flattered the collection.

"Would you like something to drink? Tea or coffee?"

We shook our heads.

"No? Well, then, sit down and tell me what you think of our lake."

Sam and I sat on the sofa and I smiled at her. "It's lovely! You're so fortunate to live here."

"Most of the time," she said, a shadow crossing her features.

"Chuck Atwell is stuck in Houston," Sam said, "so he asked us to check the house and see if we could learn anything about his missing boat. You have a good view of his dock. Did you see anyone on the property or around the boat?"

"I'm afraid not. I don't usually gaze at the lake. I'm more interested in people and collectibles."

The room bore out her statement. Porcelain dolls, a bisque collection of ballet dancers, and a lovely group of Swarovski crystal animals and birds were placed to draw the eye. Her collections were much more expensive than the trinkets Alice amassed.

I stood and walked toward a collection of crystal figurines. "You have lovely things."

She followed. "My sister Gwen loves to help me decorate the house." She pointed to the swans. "They're so graceful. I wish we had some on the lake. The mallards are beautiful, though. So peaceful."

Did her collections replace something missing from her life? "Does your husband like them? I hear he loves the water."

She shrugged one shoulder. "Only if he's fishing. He's out there now. It'll be dark soon. I hope he makes it back for the homeowners' meeting. Are you going?"

I nodded. "Could I use your powder room before we leave?"

She pointed. "Down the hall, that way."

In the hall, a photograph of three people was displayed on the wall. A young Verna and Alice stood on either side of a young man who must be Max Weller.

Verna intrigued me. There was more to her than just collecting. I couldn't put my finger on it, something a little sad? I wanted to know more. Although I couldn't very well traipse through her house, people's bathrooms were revealing.

I went in and locked the door. The walls were decorated with lovely miniature paintings flawlessly arranged. The curtain draping the bathtub looked hand-painted. On the sink lay the shell soap dish... the one from Alice's collection. Verna, Max, and Alice had an interesting relationship.

My feet started itching—it happens when curiosity overwhelms me—and kept it up until I opened the medicine cabinet. The usual array of drugstore products clustered beside an inordinate amount of barbiturates.

When I walked out, Verna and Sam were already at the front door.

"I bet Max sleeps well after all that fishing," I said.

"I wish," she sighed. "He has trouble dealing with memories from Vietnam, but he has remedies to cope with it."

"We'll see you at the meeting, then," Sam said.

She smiled. "Hopefully, Max will be with me."

* * * * *

In the car, Sam and I compared notes.

"I think Verna is a perfectionist," I said. "It must be hard for her to live on a lake that floods periodically."

"I imagine so. I asked her if Max has a key to Chuck's boat," Sam said. "They aren't close friends, she said, but Chuck could well have given him one."

We pulled up to Art Lively's house. I decided to tell Sam about my bathroom discoveries later. I wasn't sure he'd appreciate my snooping.

# FOUR

Chuck's friend met us at the door. "You must be Sam and Aggie. Come in. Friends of Chuck are friends of mine. I'm Art Lively, host for this illustrious group. Let me introduce you to the river rats and get you something to drink. Beer? Wine?"

"Beer for me," Sam said.

"White wine, please."

He led us to a stooped man with piercing blue eyes under snow-white hair. A woman about his age stood by his side.

"This man's been on the lake the longest: Gunther Schmidt." Art went to get our drinks.

Gunther studied us and grasped Sam's hand with gnarled fingers. "You two youngsters moving here, are you?"

"It's beautiful," I said. "I'd love to live here."

"This river can be treacherous. This is my wife, Ida."

"It's nice to meet you," Sam said. "This is my girlfriend, Aggie Mundeen."

I smiled and nodded. It was hard to fathom Gunther's dire description of this lazy river.

"We're just visiting," Sam said. "Chuck Atwell invited us to use his house this weekend."

"Ah. Chuck's house. Well, it's higher than most. It's gonna rain buckets, you know."

"He worries," Ida said, rolling her eyes. "He worries about everything."

Art returned with our drinks.

"After sweeping two feet of water out of our house twice in the '70s," Gunther said, "and practically rebuilding it later, when it rains, I worry. We need to move away from the water, Ida, back to New Braunfels. On a nice high spot near the family." She patted his shoulder.

"Dessert will make us all feel better," Art said, nudging the Schmidts toward a table laden with strudel, Black Forest cake, and chocolate chip cookies. On the way to the dessert table, he stopped to chat with Verna Weller and a woman with her. The man with them must be Max. Stocky, with leathered skin, he wore khakis, flat-heeled boots and a shirt with the sleeves rolled up. He looked dressed for the outdoors, not for an evening neighborhood gathering.

Sam smiled at me. "Are you hungry?"

"Not especially. I'm more interested sizing up the people."

Verna, Max, and her friend approached.

"I'm Max Weller," he said. "Sorry I missed you earlier. You've met my wife, Verna. This is her sister, Gwen Highsmith."

She was a darker blond, sturdier than Verna, but with the same engaging smile. She looked a few years older than Verna. Sam introduced us.

"Have you lived on the lake a long time?" I asked.

"I've had a cottage out here since the '80s," Max said. "Verna came out when I married her in '89."

"Where did you live before?" Sam asked Verna.

"In Seguin," Verna said, "near Gwen. I taught in the same school where Gwen is the school nurse. But after Bob died—my first husband—I quit teaching. I got awfully lonesome until I met Max." Gwen patted Verna's arm and scowled at Max.

"Swept her off her feet." Max laughed. "Sold my little fishing cabin and talked her into moving back into her and Bob's lake house. I fixed it up real nice. Didn't know she'd get all scared about livin' there."

"You didn't see this river rise in '87, Max. Bob and I lived through that flood." She looked up at Max, eyes wide. The memory frightened her, even now. She turned back to us.

"After that, I couldn't wait to get back to Seguin. Then Bob got sick and died and it didn't seem to matter where I lived."

Gwen shook her head.

Max raised supplicant hands. "I got me a boat and a thousand bucks worth of fishing gear. How am I gonna get out on the water and fish every day living in a goldern subdivision in the middle of town?"

Verna sighed. "I guess you're not."

They obviously had this conversation before. Did Max Weller love fishing enough to "borrow" Chuck's boat?

Garner Sledge sauntered up, leading with his stomach. "I've been telling you to let me modernize that house, Maxwell. Or I could build one on another lot, high up on piers out of the floodway, for you and the little lady."

"I bet you could, Garner," Max said. "You'd build me a house that cost a fortune." He looked at us and jerked his chin toward the other man. "This here is Garner Sledge."

"We met earlier." Sam's voice was neutral.

Garner didn't miss a beat. "I could build you a first-class riverside retreat, Max. Verna could quit fretting and you could keep fishing."

Max shook his head, threw up his hands and walked away. Verna and Gwen followed, like ducklings.

Garner hulked close to Sam, grabbed Sam's hand with his paw and pumped it. "Good to see you again."

Irritated by Max's aggressive stance, Sam planted his feet and straightened. I wished Sam could reveal he was an SAPD detective.

"Nice place Chuck's got there," Garner said. "Beautiful lot. I could build him a real showplace on that site."

"I don't think Chuck is interested in building a bigger house."

Max Weller, five steps away, pivoted around. "You'd like that, wouldn't you, Garner? A Houston exec could line your pockets real nice."

Garner waved Max and his insult away. "You gotta forgive Max," he told us. "He's always grousing about something." He studied his empty glass. "Think I'll get me a refill. Let me know if you wanna build a house down here. It's great living on a lake."

He winked and lumbered toward the bar. Garner loved living on the lake but didn't like to fish. Odd. Maybe it was a ruse, so nobody would suspect him of taking Chuck's boat.

Art Lively came over. "I see you've met the natives. I thought you might like to meet someone who's thinking of moving here. This is Rick Crane. Excuse me while I check the food."

Sam extended his hand. "Sam Vanderhoven. This is my girlfriend, Aggie Mundeen. She and I are here checking on Chuck Atwell's house. Do you know Chuck?"

"I met him once. Nice guy."

"So you're thinking of buying here?" I asked.

He smiled. "Maybe. I move around a lot. I'm a Game Warden for Guadalupe County, but I also cover Comal, Gonzales, and part of Bexar County."

Rick's sandy red hair was straight-cut across the top, neat, like a soldier's. His eyes, so dark brown you couldn't distinguish the pupils, contrasted with his ruddy complexion.

"You guys must see just about everything," Sam said.

"Our responsibilities include wildlife and fisheries, land and water, but we never know what we're going to find. My partner and I discovered a major drug lab the other day. If there's any kind of problem on the river, the Sheriff calls me or Joe Ramirez."

Sam leaned in close. "I'm not advertising it, but I'm a detective with SAPD. Chuck asked me to investigate the theft of his boat. Know anything about it?"

Rick raised an eyebrow. "I know it was stolen, but that's it."

"He apparently gave his boat key to a couple of neighbors. Know anything about that?"

"No. People who have second homes on the lakes do it in case of a flood, but it's kind of risky."

"That's what I thought," Sam said. "We ought to share war stories some time."

Rick nodded. "Sounds good."

"You know most of the people on Lake Placid?"

"Here and on Lake McQueeney. I live in Seguin, but I'm looking at property on the river."

"Then you probably know Garner Sledge."

"I met Sledge before at a homeowners' meeting." He took a drink, then set his jaw.

"Sounds like Max Weller's got his number," Sam said.

"Most people around here are on to Garner."

Sam nodded.

Art Lively clapped his hands and got everybody's attention.

"Time to get started," he said. "The first items on the agenda are garbage pickup and spraying pecan trees for webworms." It was clear that this lake and these people were Art's dominion.

Sam looked at me. "Ready to go?"

"Yes."

He turned to Rick. "Nice meeting you. Hope to see you around."

"Same here, Sam. Keep in touch. If I learn anything about Chuck's boat, I'll let you know." They exchanged cards.

We caught Art's eye, mouthed "Thanks," and let ourselves out.

* * * * *

Sam drove the short distance to our cottage. We had left lights on outside the houses so we could see to cross the patio. We went inside and had dinner, then settled into wrought iron spring chairs on the patio and gazed at the water.

"The air is so thick with moisture, it feels dense enough to cut," Sam said.

I leaned my head back and closed my eyes. "The south-east breeze feels good."

"It's rippling the water. Look!"

I looked in time to see a bass leap and the circle of water where he plunged back in. I gazed at lights Chuck had installed high in the trees near the lake. "I love the way those lights shine on the dock and water."

"They'll go off after midnight." Sam peered out over the lake. "I wonder if Chuck's boat is out there somewhere." He turned to me. "What did you think of the people we met today?"

"I liked most of them. Art seems to know everybody. I wonder if Chuck gave him a boat key."

"I'll find out when I call him."

"There's something else. A soap dish from Alice's collection was in Verna's bathroom. Alice said she gave it to Chuck. When it showed up at Verna's, Alice didn't ask why. And Verna and Max Weller have a ton of barbiturates in their medicine cabinet."

"You shouldn't snoop in people's cabinets."

"I'm a curious private citizen."

"Yes, but I'm a cop investigating a crime. If the Wellers have anything to do with it, a judge would throw that information out. It could ruin the case."

"I'm sorry, Sam."

He lowered his head and looked at me over his glasses. "I know you mean well. Just check with me before you forge ahead."

"I should have. I forgot." I had promised him I would, but my overwhelming curiosity was a strong force.

"Didn't Verna say Max has trouble sleeping because of trauma from Vietnam?" he said.

"That's what she *said*."

Somebody started playing music across the river, and we bounced our chairs to the beat. I could spend every evening by this river.

"By the way," he opened his palm, "when I checked the stanchions, I found this clam shell on the dock. They burrow into the lake bottom and catch food coming by. I think I'll leave it in one of the shadow boxes outside the guest house as a memento of our visit." He took my hand and pulled over to kiss me. "It's so muggy out here. Let's go inside."

While I got ready for bed, he turned on television. When I entered the living room, he was leaning forward on his knees, eyes glued to the TV screen.

*Heavy rains have produced flooding in parts of San Antonio, New Braunfels, and San Marcos.*

San Antonio footage showed cars in Sunset Ridge Shopping Center stalled in water above their tires. I looked outside. It wasn't even raining. I turned back to the TV, which showed two feet of water rushing down New Braunfels Avenue. Burr Road, where Grace and I lived, dead-ended into New Braunfels Avenue. My throat tightened.

"Could water reach our houses?" I grabbed my phone to call Grace. There was no answer. "I think her neighbor on the other side is out of town." I looked pleadingly at Sam. "I don't know anybody else. Can you call an officer to go check on her?"

"SAPD will be swamped rescuing people who drove their cars into low-water crossings. It happens every time it rains. I doubt there's a problem from New Braunfels going uphill on Burr Road."

"We're not that far up the hill." I stared at the screen.

*Ingredients for heavy rain have come together for the weekend. The only part of the puzzle missing is what triggering mechanism will bring heavier rain. The mostly likely trigger is a cold front to the west, which should arrive in south Texas late Saturday or Saturday night.*

I dialed Grace's number again. Why didn't she answer? She was self-sufficient, but except for her beloved terrier, Boffo, she lived alone.

"I don't think we need to worry," Sam said. "But I guess we'll have to stay inside." He bent to kiss me, wrapped his arms around me and nuzzled my neck. "We'll see what the weather's like in the morning and call Grace. I'm sure she's all right."

I wanted to believe him. And I wanted him to keep nuzzling my neck.

# FIVE

## RICK CRANE

Game Warden Rick Crane couldn't sleep. He had stayed at the homeowner's meeting as long as he could stand the blather before he sneaked out. He liked Art Lively, but Art was an insurance agent and programmed to give a sales pitch every time he opened his mouth. He got up the weekly poker game, though, which was a big plus in his favor.

As soon as Rick left Art's house, he looked at the sky. It looked heavy, like it was about to disgorge itself into the lake. He muttered to himself. He'd seen that kind of sky before, ominous skies over coastal waters where he'd done plenty of salt-water rescues.

After college and attending Texas A&M's Game Warden Academy, he worked fifteen years on all kinds of boats in the Gulf of Mexico near Galveston, Rockport, and Port O'Connor. Seguin was his first inland assignment. It was hard to imagine the lazy Guadalupe River causing havoc like the Gulf, but the river was swollen and angry. It was unmistakable—the look of water and sky that made you edgy.

The phone rang, rousing him from a deep sleep. He rolled over and glanced at the clock. Five a.m. Not a time for good news. He stared at the neon numbers and picked up the receiver. "Rick Crane."

"This is Joe. The Sheriff just called. The lakes are going to flood. He wants us to get the boat out of the barn and head to Lake McQueeney to evacuate people."

"Lake McQueeney is too big for two men in a boat to cover."

"Yeah, I know," Joe said. "But we're all he's got."

The only law enforcement officers with water rescue training, he and Joe Ramirez were used to hearing from the Sheriff. Rick would rather work with Joe than anybody. Before college, Joe served as a Marine in Viet Nam and trained as a Game Warden at Texas A&M College Station. Like Rick, he'd worked on fishing boats, oyster boats, and shrimpers, rocking and reeling in the Gulf. Together, the two hotshots in their thirties had plenty of rough water experience. But they never expected to need it as Game Wardens in Seguin, Texas.

Lake McQueeney was the largest body of water downstream from Canyon Lake. Treasure Island, an oasis of luxury homes in the middle of Lake McQueeney, connected to the mainland by a short bridge.

"We can start with Treasure Island," Rick said.

"People won't want to abandon those homes," Joe said, "high water or not."

"Yeah. I know. I'll meet you at the boat barn."

They got Rick's assigned craft out of the barn at McQueeney, an eighteen-footer with a one-hundred-fifty Mercury outboard motor he used to patrol the waterways. They trailered the boat behind Rick's pickup and drove to the already-flooded Raccoon Golf Course above McQueeney.

"I never thought we'd be boating on the golf course," Joe said.

They launched in water covering the course and steered the boat into the lake.

"I'm glad to see daylight," Rick said.

They approached each house and shouted through a megaphone: "All residents need to evacuate. Drive off the island to higher ground."

People grabbed belongings and started their cars.

"Some of them are leaving," said Joe.

Others yelled back. "We've seen rain before. We're staying put."

Rick and Joe motored to the next house. More rain fell in late morning as they circled Treasure Island. They kept at it for several hours, with the water still rising.

"I wonder if the empty houses will be here next weekend when the owners return," Rick said.

At dusk, they left McQueeney and hauled the eighteen-footer toward the low side of Lake Placid, downstream from Lake McQueeney. The sky darkened, and rain fell harder.

Rick looked at Joe. "This is going to get a lot worse."

# SIX

## AGGIE MUNDEEN

Startled by a voice, I woke, blinked and sat up.

*"I love the colors in these tiles: red, blue, lavender, gold. I wish you could see them, Aggie. When I finish, this table will look like the sunset."* There was a pause. *"I'm glad to see you're happy."*

My heart pounded. It was Grace, talking in a clear, calm voice, describing tables she was tiling. I loved her like an older sister or a mother. Since my parents died young, and my aunt and uncle were gone now, too, Grace was my rock. She had suffered through tragedies in her life—the loss of three husbands. But instead of embittering her, loss had made her wise. Being impulsive, I relied on her sensible, thoughtful counsel. But why would I hear her voice? Had I dreamed it?

I looked over at Sam. He slept peacefully, emitting an occasional snore. I closed my eyes. What did Grace say? "I'm glad you're happy?"

Earlier in the week, I told her Sam promised to check his friend's lake house and would ask if we could stay the weekend. Once we made plans, in my flurry to grocery shop and pack, I forgot to tell Grace I was leaving. How could she know we went to the lake or if I was happy? I could be shopping or with another friend. With our garage doors closed, it was hard to tell if we were home or not.

Fully awake, I knew I'd never go back to sleep. I rose quietly and tiptoed in bare feet on cold Saltillo tiles from the bedroom to the living room. As quietly as I could, I unlocked the patio door. The screen door only creaked once as I glided through. Curling into a wrought iron patio chair, I pulled my feet up under me and peered out over the lake. Moisture-laden air felt like a lid pressing down over the water. Wind gusts periodically burst through, trying to dislodge the oppressive blanket.

I gazed down the sloping lawn to undulating black water. The tree lights were off. It must be after midnight because only moonlight shone on our dock. I couldn't even see the rungs of the ladder. Across the lake, most dock lights were off. Focusing on the few still lighted, I studied circles they projected on the lake. The water looked blacker. Thicker. Faster-moving. I stuck out my tongue to feel the weight of the air. Heavy rains were coming. I inhaled deeply, relishing the thought of our glorious, private, stay-inside rainy weekend. No crime. No pressure. No disruption.

Sam creaked through the screen door and stood on the patio. "Couldn't sleep?"

"I had a dream. Grace was talking to me about tiling tables."

He sat in the chair beside me. "That's random."

"I know. I've never dreamed about her before."

"You're in a strange place. Maybe dreaming about her is comforting."

I smiled at him. "I'm very comforted. I'm exactly where I belong."

He reached over and squeezed my hand.

Distant lightning flashed, illuminating a dock across the river. Two people in hooded jackets stood face-to-face on the dock, gesturing and shouting.

I pointed. "Do you see them?"

He leaned forward in his chair. "Is that the Wellers?"

"I can't tell if they're men or woman, or even if that's the Wellers' house."

Angry voices carried across the water, distorted by the rumble of distant thunder.

"I can't make out what they're saying."

"No," he said, "but they're plenty mad about something."

We walked to the edge of the patio and squinted across the lake. "Maybe I should go over there," he said.

"I didn't hear any cries for help."

"I'll get my Streamlight." He hustled to his car for the flashlight and raced back across the patio as lightning flashed. He shined his light across the water and scanned the dock and water. The people were gone.

Sam lowered the light. "They must have gone inside to finish their argument. I'll drive over there later this morning and check a couple of houses. Make sure everybody's all right."

"And I'll call Grace to tell her we're here and make sure she's okay."

The air was dense with moisture like a saturated sponge. We settled in, staring across the lake at the empty dock. We must have dozed off in our chairs, because when I woke, the first streaks of daylight penetrated bulging clouds. I let Sam sleep until the sky grew lighter. Then I went inside to make coffee, knowing the creak of the screen door would wake him. I brought coffee mugs to the patio so we could sip and watch the sky brighten. I loved how each day was newly born. Daybreak was the first sunrise over water I watched with Sam.

"Chuck's probably awake by now. I'll call him," he said.

I went back inside long enough to scramble eggs and brought food to the patio table so we could watch the day unfold. "What did Chuck say?"

"He gave a boat key to Garner, Max Weller, and Art, so they could get his boat out if the water rose. He didn't think any of them would steal it."

"Hmm. Probably not. I keep thinking about those people arguing," I said. "They could have fallen in the lake and been swept downstream. Nobody would see them."

"Seems like we would have heard something from here... a cry for help. A splash."

I nodded.

* * * * *

Mid-morning, it began to sprinkle. Lake dwellers across the water started dragging lawn furniture inside. There was no activity at the house where the twosome vanished. People climbed into boats and headed upriver, struggling to maintain power against the current, and dodging tree limbs and debris washed into the lake.

"They must be going to the slip under I-10 to get their boats out of the river," Sam said. "I'll check the weather." We went inside. While I loaded the dishwasher, he clicked on a San Antonio TV station.

*Remnants of hurricanes in the Eastern Pacific bringing high-level moisture into Central Texas, combined with low-level south east moisture and strong winds coming from the Gulf of Mexico, will bring heavy rain to Central Texas. We expect an upper-level front to come from New Mexico Saturday night and Sunday and trigger heavy rainfall. We could have four to five inches, with isolated amounts up to six inches.*

It was late morning when Sam clicked off the TV. "I'm going to throw on shorts and drive to the other side of the lake to check on those people. It's pretty low over there."

I scrambled to the bedroom to dress. "I'll go with you."

"Why don't you keep an eye on the weather forecast? We're so high off the river, you're perfectly safe. I'll be back before you know it."

I nodded reluctantly. Sam was always racing toward a problem without me, an ingrained work habit. I admired him for it. But this was *our* weekend. I didn't relish spending any of it alone.

Before I could say a word, he was out the door, angling the Caprice out of the driveway onto Lake Placid Drive.

I called Grace and let the phone ring and ring and ring. There was no answer. It was nearly noon. She didn't usually have lunch outings. Where would she go?

# SEVEN

## SAM VANDERHOVEN

Sam drove out of Lake Placid Estates and turned right. When he reached the bridge over the river, he slowed to watch the boats and jet skis below, drivers doggedly grinding their motors upstream toward the boat slip at the I-10 underpass. He flipped on the radio.

*Weather conditions converging over Central Texas remind me of patterns preceding the 1972 flood that devastated Houston and Galveston.*

Past the bridge, he turned right on Turtle Lane, into Pecan Grove subdivision. All along the street, people retrieved furniture from docks and hauled it inside. Families headed for their cars.

He hadn't gone far when Turtle Lane dipped, and two feet of water covered the road. Would his low-slung Caprice make it through? He remembered the people on the dock. He pushed forward at a steady speed, trying not to slosh water into the engine.

Where had the standing water come from? Rain was just beginning to fall. He glanced at the lake. Rising lake water had made its way through saturated lawns to the road and filled the low spot. From upstream, water from Canyon Lake and Lake McQueeney must be cascading over the dams into Lake Placid.

Dark clouds looked pregnant with more rain. He looked between houses, straining to see across the lake. The cottage he shared with Aggie looked at least thirty feet higher than the spot where he was. Thank God she was high and safe.

As he neared the end of Turtle Lane, lake water seeped slowly across lawns. A man worked feverishly to get his John Deere ride-on into the garage. Was his house next to the one where the people disappeared? Rain fell steadily. Sam squinted, comparing the position of the houses to Chuck's cottages across the lake. Which house and dock belonged to the feuding pair? On the far side of Turtle Lane, another man pulled a boat and trailer to higher ground. Having secured his mower in the garage, the man sloshed through his yard and across the water-filled road toward the boat and trailer.

Sam rolled down the window. "Looks like we're in for a flood."

The man shouted back. "The TV shows San Antonio flooding. I thought I could mow the lawn before it rained here." Water poured down his face. "I've got jet skis in the garage, too. When water floods the building, I hope my equipment doesn't break out the walls."

Thirty feet from the man's house and garage, water sloshed over his retaining wall. "My friend called from McQueeney and said it's raining like hell over there," he shouted. "The dam's overflowing. Said we need to get out of here. I've got no shoes, no wallet and no phone, but I know better than to take time to get them. We're heading for higher ground." Before Sam could ask about the neighbors, the man hopped into the truck cab, and they chugged away.

Sam took a deep breath. McQueeney Dam was north of Lake Placid. Water pouring over it was flowing into Lake Placid. Lake Dunlop and Canyon Dam Reservoir were north of McQueeney. If the McQueeney dam was overflowing, water must also be cascading over Canyon Dam. And more rain was expected. Sam shuddered at the possibility: Canyon Dam could break.

He pictured Aggie back at the cottage, her liquid brown eyes wide as they flipped back and forth from the TV to the lake, swinging her gorgeous, thick brown hair. What would he do without her? He had to get back.

A Seguin police car rolled up behind him, light bar flashing. The speaker blared: "All homeowners must evacuate the area now. The river will continue to rise and flood your homes. Leave immediately!"

Sam kicked off his shoes, rolled up his pants, and splashed to the patrol car. The officer cracked his window.

Sam shook water off his face. "I'm a San Antonio Police officer—Sam Vanderhoven. What can I do to help?"

"I'm Jess Perez. You and I worked gang detail a few years back. What are you doing here?"

"Supposed to be on vacation, Jess. How can I help?"

"Best thing is to leave the area. I've knocked on doors this side of the river. Got to get these people out before the road floods and they're trapped. Then I've got to evacuate people on the other side."

"My girlfriend is over there."

"Better get her out. This river's not going to stop rising."

Sam took a deep breath. Aggie could be in danger. He splashed back to his car. Would it start? On the third try, the motor turned over. He blew out a breath, wiped his hand across his mouth and drove until he found a patch of unflooded asphalt. He turned the car around and slowed to pump the brakes, hoping they still worked. Thank God they did.

The going was slow. People had abandoned homes, dragged children, pets, and keepsakes to their cars and started a watery, precarious trip to the highway. When he reached the intersection at 90A, he turned left, hoping he could make it to Chuck's house and to Aggie.

Rain pounded the car in sheets. Lake Placid Drive was not covered with water, but he could see it seeping up from the lake through the lawns. His brakes grabbed every two seconds, and the engine struggled. Two houses before their cottage, he came up behind Jess Perez, shouting for people to evacuate.

He jumped out, rushed over, knocked on his window and pointed. "I've got to get Aggie out of that cottage. My car almost drowned out. Can we come with you? We can help evacuate people."

"Thanks, but you know I can't take a civilian in this car. She'll be in danger and slow me down. I got to get these people out of here. You get her out and head for the entrance. If your engine floods, I'll pick you up."

Sam wiped his face. Lightning crashed across the sky. "I'll get her out, but my car might not make it to the entrance. Think about what I said." He hopped into his Caprice and aimed for Chuck's driveway.

# EIGHT

## AGGIE MUNDEEN

Rain started to pour. I stared at the TV. Photographers in rain gear shot flooded areas of San Antonio: Cibolo Creek. Olmos Basin. The Quarry. Sunset Ridge. New Braunfels Avenue.

Grace didn't answer her phone.

Burr Road, where she and I lived in adjacent bungalows, sloped gradually up from New Braunfels, but our homes were not far up the incline. Water hurled down the slope, rose from New Braunfels, and rain poured like it would never stop.

I dialed her number again. Where would she go in the middle of torrential rains? I let it ring over and over. Where could she be?

My focus shifted between television and the windows looking out over Lake Placid. Was that Sam's car moving between the houses across the lake? I couldn't tell. It was impossible to see much of anything.

I couldn't see our dock. Water covered it and was creeping up the steps toward the patio. Surely the rain would stop, and the water would recede. My pulse raced. Sam wouldn't leave me if he thought I was in danger. Maybe he couldn't get back to the lake house. Should I run to Alice's and hope her green Mercury could get us away from the lake? I wanted to be with Sam, but he might have a better chance of escaping the flood without me.

A car honked. Seconds later, Sam sloshed across the patio and yanked open the door. "We have to leave. Police are evacuating the area. Houses across the river are flooded, and the water is still rising." He dripped across the floor, grabbed coats from the bedroom closet and told me to put one on.

"It's flooding in San Antonio. I called Grace... got no answer."

I ran to the kitchen, sealed my Nokia phone in a plastic bag and stuffed it down my shirt. I grabbed a huge garbage bag, raced to the bedroom and stuffed in every sweater and coat I could find, plus two blankets.

He came after me and grasped my arm. "What are you doing?"

"Somebody might need them."

"We have to leave." He hurried me and my garbage bag out the door and to his car. We could barely see the circular driveway for sheets of rain. He drove slowly up the driveway, muttering, "Where's the damned road?"

As we turned onto Lake Placid Drive, I saw Alice jump in her car. She was soaked, and her car looked like it was filled to the brim. I waved at her.

"Honk, Sam," I said.

She pulled in front of us and we followed her. Sam's engine sputtered, coughed, then caught again. Did Alice have any space left in her car?

Drenched people on both sides of the road splashed from their homes loading children, pets, and possessions into their cars. Disbelief marked their faces. Did they realize how fast the water was rising? I wanted to yell at them to hurry up. Water crept around houses and fingered toward the road. If they had watercraft tied at their docks, it was too late to save them. It seemed silly that I had been worried about losing our weekend—people could lose their lives.

"Do you see anyone without a car?" Sam said. We squinted through sheets of rain, scanning for people who needed a way out.

"No." We gawked between houses at the swirling river. Jet skis unmoored from docks floated down river. Lawn furniture and pieces of homes rushed by. Ski boats zigzagged through churning water.

"Look." he said. "Boats are still struggling to go upriver through that onslaught. I don't see how they can make it to the I-10 slip."

Rain poured harder.

We reached the Highway 90A entrance to the subdivision. A Seguin patrol officer waved people around his vehicle. Alice honked at us, pulled around him and headed for Seguin. She must have a friend or relative in town with a house on high ground. I remembered the merriment in her eyes and hoped she'd be okay. I felt a pang of longing for my San Antonio bungalow.

Sam pulled up behind the officer and turned to me. "Aggie, I need to go with the officer and try to help these people. We'll flag down somebody who's going to high ground in Seguin. You can go with them where you'll be safe. We can meet up later."

"I don't want to go with strangers and wonder where you are, Sam. I'd rather go with you."

"I don't know where Jess is going. They might send him to a flood area."

"You know him?"

"He was a San Antonio patrolman. We worked some cases together. When I saw him earlier, I was afraid my car would flood out and asked if we could go with him. He doesn't want to take you, Aggie. He can't put a civilian in danger."

"I'm certified as a life guard. After that girl drowned at the health club, I took training." It was partially true. I took classes but was never certified.

"I don't know, Aggie. This could be dangerous."

"I want to go with you, Sam." I stared at him. "Convince him I can help."

He studied my face. "Okay." He jumped out, splashed to the patrol car, and knocked on the officer's window. "We can help you, Jess." He pointed at me. "She's a trained life guard."

Through rain sheeting down his window, I saw skepticism on the officer's face.

"We can help evacuate people," Sam said.

I rolled down my window. "I can persuade women who don't want to leave their homes to evacuate."

Officer Perez glared at me, drew his hand across his mouth and threw up his hands. "All right. Drive across the highway to high ground. As soon as I make sure everybody's out of the subdivision, I'll meet you over there."

Sam splashed back to the car, and we lurched across the highway. Cars streamed out of Lake Placid and head for Seguin. A few turned left toward San Antonio. They might get stranded.

Office Perez stayed at the entrance a few minutes after the last car left, then crossed the road and pulled up beside us. "All right. Get in. We've got work to do." He looked at my garbage bag. "What's that?"

"Extra coats and sweaters." I pushed my bag across the backseat and slid in. The plastic bag stuffed in my shirt itched.

Sam hopped in the front and introduced me to Officer Perez, who grunted. His radio squawked from headquarters, "Stand by." He didn't inform dispatch he had passengers.

"They're sending me all over the place to evacuate people. They sent me to Glen Cove first. It's the lowest area in Seguin. The Guadalupe River was covering back yards on Elmwood, Wayside, Montclair, and Crescent. Thing is, unless people have relatives, there's no place to go. The school's locked up and nobody can find the custodian with the keys, so people can't get into the gymnasium."

From the amount of water rising in Lake Placid, tons of water must be overflowing dams from lakes to the north. New Braunfels was flooding, with more rain forecast. Why was there was no preparation, no local weather reports of flooding, no reporting of water heights at various places, no designated shelters, no instructions about where to go?

Perez's radio squawked. "Get over to Chaparral Country Club. People are stranded in their houses. Go west on 90A and left on FM 725."

Water seeped over Highway 90A. At the 725 intersection, we climbed a hill. Then the road sloped down, and we plowed through water. If we got to the country club, how were we going to get back? We drove into the club entrance and stopped. Rising water had flooded the golf course. Homes around the course had water eight feet high up the walls. Cows and horses perched on rooftops. On the roof of a two-story house almost completely engulfed with water, a man stood waiting for help.

"Have you got rope and flotation gear?" Sam asked.

"No. Nobody expected this. This happened so fast, there wasn't time to get anything. Chief Schneider was the only one who even remembered the '72 flood," Jess said. "Nobody knew it could get this bad."

That poor man on his roof. How terrified he must be, so alone. I knew what that was like. After Lester the Louse seduced me at age eighteen and took off, I was alone and scared. After a while, being alone seemed better than a risky entanglement. I had yearned for a caring relationship for a long time. Too long.

I strained to see through the deluge. One boat, then two, cut through the water. Then more. Men appeared from all directions in private water craft and started rescuing people from roofs. They threw ropes to stranded victims and hauled them into their boats, risking their own safety.

At the edge of the water, a big dump truck sat on higher ground. The boats dropped off their passengers and motored back into the angry water, searching for someone else who needed help. Whenever a boat got close to us, I cracked the window and called out we had a coat or blanket for the victims. Some of the boat drivers with a passenger would inch closer to pick one up, put the boat in neutral and have the passenger steady the boat with an oar while they reached out to collect a coat.

Deep water was slowly creeping higher, threatening us.

"Jess, can you back up and get us to higher ground?" Sam said.

Jess turned around. "Water's starting to cover the road behind us."

We were stranded just beyond the reach of rising water. Sam and Jess weren't programmed to ask for help, and we were unable to help anyone else. Nobody would think to rescue us from a police car. We looked official.

I put my hands on Sam's shoulders and leaned up to his ear. "I love you, Sam."

He squeezed my hand. "I love you, too."

The water was incredibly swift. Trees and pieces of debris rushed by us. The dump truck filled with people, and water rose up its sides at an alarming rate. Houses bordering the golf course began to topple.

"Let's call for one of the men in a boat to pick us up," I said.

I was too late. The boat brigade had rescued everyone but us and disappeared. The fear of abandonment rose in my throat. A wave of water washed over the cab of the dump truck and drowned the engine.

Were we going to die?

# NINE

## RICK CRANE

Rick Crane and Joe Ramirez plowed down Highway 90A, their boat and trailer splashing through water. It was growing dark as they veered on to Turtle Lane toward the low side of Lake Placid. Rain fell in sheets. They scanned both sides of the lane for somebody stranded or trying to move on foot through the deluge.

"I don't see anybody, do you?" Joe said.

Rick shook his head. Most of the houses were dark. A few had lights on, but no one waved from windows. They honked and took turns cracking a window to shout through the megaphone. There was no response. These houses looked like abandoned relics waiting for rising water. Rick hoped the people had evacuated.

Once they left the truck cab, they couldn't see anything without their spotlight. At the end of Turtle Lake, they launched the boat over submerged ground. Rick had never seen water rise this fast.

Rick started the motor and steered into the lake, looking for people trapped in flooded houses. Life jackets lay stacked on the floor of the boat alongside piles of coiled rope. Joe navigated, swinging the spotlight in a horizontal arc to watch for flotsam. Logs and debris could cripple or sink their boat. In the lake, water sloshed over rooftops.

"What's that? A power line!" Rick yelled. Electric lines loomed at eye level in front of them.

"Hope it's dead!" Joe pushed it up with a paddle. They held their breath as the boat slid underneath. Their boat had plenty of metal parts to conduct electricity.

Lightning flashed. "Open water is the worst place to be in this storm," Rick shouted. Another line loomed up so fast they didn't see it.

"Watch out!" Joe called. They ducked. Their boat slipped under the line by inches.

Rick shook his head. "We barely missed that one."

Joe shined his spotlight over the water. Floating wreckage bobbed toward the boat—jet skis, propane tanks, furniture, fencing, boats, automobiles, docks, pieces of houses. Rubbish from both sides of the river careened downriver toward the dam. To dodge oncoming debris, Rick ran back out of the current to find quieter water.

A thud rocked the boat and the engine cut out. The boat listed to port.

"What the hell?" Joe bent over the stern. "A log is lodged in the propeller." He grabbed the crowbar they carried to dislodge debris and push the boat out of shallow water.

Rick stuck a paddle in the current to try to stabilize the boat while Joe straddled the stern, kicked the log, and prodded it with the crowbar.

"Got to get it out." He kicked and kicked until the log finally drifted off. He dragged himself onboard. "Okay." He blew out a breath. "Try the motor." After a few sputters, it started.

They resumed the search, shining the spotlight and listening for shouts.

"Hear that?" Rick said.

A man called for help. He was standing on the top of his RV. Only the top two feet of his vehicle were visible. The rest of it had sunk under water. They maneuvered close enough to throw him a life jacket tied to a rope.

"Put the jacket on and hold on to the rope," Rick shouted. "I've got it tied to the boat. I'm going to drift downstream, wait for you to float toward us and pull you in."

Panic crossed the man's face.

Rick drifted downstream. Facing upstream, he powered up the motor to steady the boat against the current.

"I hope he can hold on," Joe said. When the man floated close enough, Joe pulled him in with the rope and made him comfortable in the boat.

"Look over there," Rick said.

Several RVs had come unmoored and were floating down-river. Rick and Joe shouted at the RVs through the megaphone. There was no answer. The RVs would go over the dam and crash into the stream below. Anyone inside was going to die.

A woman screamed.

"Back there!" Joe said.

She leaned from the window of her floating trailer home. Her home was lighter and not yet waterlogged. As they drew closer, it began to sink.

"I think she's too large to fit through the window," Rick said.

"Water is already barricading the door," Joe said.

They pulled cautiously up to the RV. Rick struggled to stabilize the boat while Joe grabbed the crowbar and ripped the window apart. The woman squirmed out the opening and landed in a heap in the boat.

"Thank you, thank you," she kept saying as Joe settled her on the boat floor.

They paused, listening for more cries for help. Nothing but silence. Though the black sky, they shined the spotlight in the direction they hoped was land.

"I don't see anything but water," Rick said.

Joe pointed. "I think there were houses over there. Water must have shoved them off the foundations and pushed them over the dam."

Rick steered the struggling boat upriver. He saw lights, heard voices and turned the boat in that direction. Figures waved flashlights.

"Look!" he shouted. "My truck is up there."

Rick's truck, on an elevated knoll, was surrounded by people. Other truck drivers had gathered there to pick up survivors. Displaced people steadily moved to higher ground. Rick gauged the rising water. He'd have to move his truck father up the slope and hope he parked it high enough.

As they unloaded their passengers, a man walked up to Rick.

"Dave Kelley." He stuck out his hand. "I'm a volunteer fireman. What can I do to help?"

"Rick Crane. Can you stay with my vehicle and trailer and move it up ahead of the rising water?"

"Sure. My truck is high and dry on the overpass at I-10. I came down here with a friend."

"I've got a landing light mounted on the roof," Rick said. "If you shine the spotlight into the air periodically, it will give me a location to steer toward." He didn't want to leave his vehicle with the spotlight on. The battery would eventually run down and cut off his only communication with the Sheriff's Department. "After we're back in the river, get people with flashlights to turn them on every so often."

Dave Kelley nodded. "I'll do it."

Rick threw him the keys. Dave caught them, nodded, and steered the soaking passengers toward safety.

Rick and Joe aimed their boat back into the black, rampant river.

# TEN

Back on the water, in total darkness and pouring rain, they had no idea where they were. They scanned with the light, trying to find the place where they'd gone under the power line. The water was still rising.

"I think we're *above* the power lines," Joe said. If the propeller hit a single live line, they'd be electrocuted.

Rick had to guess where the lines were, cut the motor, paddle away and hope they were out of reach. They felt a nudge under the boat.

"I think we crossed over a line," Joe said.

They looked at each other. They might not make it out.

Rick cocked his head. "You hear that?"

"Yeah. Over there!"

Joe swung the spotlight around, the watery light picking out waving shapes. Four adults and several children were trapped in a slowly sinking house. Moving against the current, Rick inched toward the swaying structure. If the current threw the boat hard against the house, they'd all be lost. Even if they managed to steady the boat, there were too many people to carry safely. They would overload the boat and risk disaster.

"We'll have to get one group to high ground and try to get back for the others," he said, throwing life jackets to those who were staying behind.

Rick tried to stabilize the rocking boat. Joe helped two children into the boat with two adults to keep hold of them.

"Put your life jackets on and don't stand," he said. He called to the others still in the house. "Make sure your life jackets are securely fastened. Stay as still as you can and hold onto each other. We'll be back."

Rick turned the boat into the river. "Can you see the light?" Joe asked.

"Not yet." Rick turned upriver, scanning for land. He spotted the beam from the roof of his truck, saw flashlights, heard voices and aimed the boat toward the sound.

Dave stood by his truck. Rick steered as close as he could to high ground, then idled the boat. Men waded up to get the passengers and lead them out of the water to safety.

Rick and Joe turned the boat back into the river. They had to find the rest of the people trapped in the house.

Rick struggled to steer. "The water's rising and moving faster!"

"Hear that?" Joe yelled.

Rick heard people shouting and turned the boat toward the sound.

"Help us! Help us. The house is sinking."

"Stay close together. We're coming!"

Rick eased the boat up to the swaying house.

"We've got you," Joe shouted, grabbing the hands of a child and adult.

Rick idled the motor and reached for the other two. They got them into the boat fast as they could.

"Hang on," Rick said, returning to the motor. "I've got to get this boat away from the house."

They made it barely outside the churn of water. Sucking a swoosh of water inward, the house sank.

The children and adults cried, huddled in the bottom of the boat. Rick searched the sky for the spotlight. With the water continuing to rise, its location had changed.

"There it is," Joe shouted.

Focused on the light, they followed the glow back to the rescue spot, the patch of road on higher ground. The passengers clambered off the boat and out of deep water. Once on the rise, they could make their way safely toward Highway 90.

"I'll stay with the boat," Joe said. "You check things on land."

Rick slogged toward his truck where Dave Kelley had moved it to higher ground. He thanked Dave and jumped into the cab to radio the Sheriff's Department.

"A lot of houses went over the dam," Rick said. "On our last run, we didn't hear any more cries for help."

A volunteer brought him a sandwich and drink. Sitting still for the first time in hours, Rick realized how tired he was. He saw another volunteer trudging through water, carrying food and drink to Joe in the boat.

"This thing isn't over," the sheriff said.

"Yeah. I know."

They had to make more runs into the river. At least the rain had let up some. He got a gas can out of the bed, shook it, and carried the half-full can toward the boat.

"Good thing we have that," Joe said, refilling the tank. "Ready to go?"

"Yep."

Throughout Saturday night, they made numerous runs into the river. When they returned to an area where they previously rescued someone, the house would be gone. They lost count of how many people they retrieved. Nearing exhaustion, they motored toward the pick-up area.

# ELEVEN

## AGGIE MUNDEEN

We sat for so long in Jess Perez's patrol car, it must be well past midnight Saturday. Jess had a search light, so we could see the water rising up the side of the dump truck. The rain had lightened. If the water didn't get too much higher, the people in the truck would probably be safe. I wasn't so sure about us. How high did the water have to get to float our car?

"I'm looking for trees to climb, just in case," I said.

"Good," Sam said. "We might be able to grab some debris, float to a tree, and climb out of the water."

The men would be able to do that. Did I have enough upper-body strength? I would certainly try. I tried to think of an alternate escape plan and couldn't come up with anything.

Jess stayed connected to dispatch and asked for rescue.

I thought of Grace. Where could she be? What was she going through?

Sam rolled down his window and leaned out to gauge the water. "It's six inches up on the tires," he said.

I buried my face in the back of Sam's shirt.

He reached back and patted my shoulder. "It's going to be okay."

I kissed his neck. I didn't think any of us were going to be okay.

Perez got a garbled message from dispatch and sat up straight. "The Texas Guard is heading our way with some type of transport."

We waited and waited, scanning the river for trees to climb and watching for floating debris. Spotlighting trees gave us something to do in the interminable dark night.

We heard a powerful rumbling sound in the distance. Too excited to stay in the car, we eased out the windows. The rain had lightened. Sam helped me onto the hood with my bag. Jess climbed onto the roof.

Crouched in the rain, we shined our light at a huge green vehicle topping a rise. Thirty feet long and fifteen feet high, it inched toward us on mammoth tires and lumbered into the water. When the amphibious vehicle pulled up next to the dump truck, we saw that the saviors wore Army uniforms. Passengers from the disabled truck climbed into the bed of the massive Army vehicle. It lurched over to us and we crawled in, soaked and grateful. The life jackets they gave us were damp but warm. We distributed the coats and blankets we had left to shivering people. We might not die after all.

The ponderous Army vehicle operated by Texas National Guardsmen carried us back to 725 and onto Highway 90A. We passed the entrance to Lake Placid Estates. Just past the 90A bridge, we slowed and labored onto Turtle Lane. Close to the highway, the road was stable, the first non-flooded riverside land I'd seen since yesterday. We rumbled down Turtle Lane toward the low-lying areas.

Our vehicle stopped on high ground where more military trucks loaded with people were starting their motors. Our driver leaned out and yelled to the other drivers. "Where should we take our passengers?"

We breathed relieved sighs and pumped the hands of the Guardsmen who stood nearby. "Thank you so much!"

They shrugged and smiled and acted like they rescued stranded people in the middle of the night all the time.

Close by, in the shallowest part of the still-raging river, two men unloaded passengers from their boat.

Sam leaned out of our flatbed. "Isn't that the Game Warden we met at the meeting? Hey, Rick."

Close to us, the water looked shallow. An excited child squirmed out of his mother's arms and jumped off our vehicle. He screamed as the current swept him off his feet.

"Hang on!" Sam jumped in after him, reaching for the boy but losing his footing, going down hard.

"Sam!" I climbed over the edge and followed.

The water was deeper than it looked. A Guardsman lunged toward the boy and scooped him up. Sam got to his feet but just as I reached him, he stumbled and fell. We both lost our footing and were carried away into the churning water.

# TWELVE

People screamed, "Somebody's in the river!"

Sam and I were caught in a current, helpless, pushed across the dark river.

Even wearing life jackets, it was hard to keep our heads above the roiling water. Lights onshore highlighted Rick Crane. He charged to his boat and vaulted over the side. The man with him started the engine and turned the boat into the raging water. Thank God they saw us.

Moonlight outlined debris bobbing our way.

I yelled to Sam. "Turn your feet upriver. We can kick to deflect the debris!"

"I'm trying to turn, Aggie. Hang on!"

The beam from the boat's floodlight cut through the darkness. Thankfully, they were downstream. If they were upriver and tried to come close, their motor could displace enough water to nudge us toward the dam.

They scanned the water with their light, back and forth across the lake, all the way to the far side. The beam picked up land points jutting into the lake that had snagged debris floating past. Piles of refuse had spread into dark, impenetrable patches. If we could get to one of those patches, maybe we could grab onto something.

"Sam, are you kicking toward the other bank? We can hang onto something over there."

"I'm kicking!"

A splintered corner of a house headed straight at Sam. Looking toward shore, he didn't see it coming.

"Watch out!" I screamed.

It hit him. I heard him cry out, and he went under.

"Sam! Are you okay?" Breathless from kicking, my voice was reedy. "Sam?"

The current swept away the debris. Sam popped up out of the water, closer to the other shore. I kicked harder. I finally got close enough to see that he floated face up, his head flooded with moonlight. His eyes were closed.

"Sam. Sam. Can you hear me?"

"I hear you, Aggie." His voice was weak. "Whatever hit me broke my arm." He moaned. "My ribs...."

I grabbed the back of his life jacket. I'd have to pull him to the side of the lake. I got on my back beside him, grasped the back of his jacket with one hand, churned water with the other and kicked like crazy. Buoyed by water, he was light. When we finally reached a debris pile on the other side, I was panting and running out of steam.

The tangle of refuse looked safe enough, but I couldn't distinguish everything on it. Or see under it. There could be snakes.

The adjacent pile was covered with what looked like a section of upturned roof. Floating on top of a tangle of weeds and debris, the structure looked like it could support us. If I could get us on it, we'd be out of the cold water.

"Okay," I said. "We made it. I'm going to get on that upturned roof and pull you up with me."

I clutched Sam's jacket and kicked until we reached the pile. I scooted up sideways on the upturned planks, pausing to test them. I didn't want to end up falling into the water underneath, entwined in a snarl of refuse, unable to surface and unable to cling to Sam.

The roof seemed stable, so I started pulling him up. He grimaced every time he moved. What if I made his injury worse? What if the blow had a punctured lung? What if he was bleeding internally?

I shook my head, trying to dispel my fear. I had to get us out of the water. I scooted farther up and tugged more gently.

He moaned a little, but I was making progress. I edged up in increments until I had my whole body and half of his on the upturned roof.

He didn't speak, and his eyes were closed. Somehow, I had to stabilize the top half of his body and let go of his jacket long enough to get his legs up on the planks. I nudged him next to the roof joist and gently pushed him against it.

"I hope I'm not hurting you, Sam." I leaned over him. "Are you awake?"

"I'm okay. Very sleepy."

He must be foggy from trauma. He didn't seem to be hurting. I thought I could get his legs up, one at a time. He emitted a few moans, but I did it.

Gripping his life jacket, I lay back on the roof beside him, exhausted. The stars seemed higher in the sky than I remembered, the moonlight pale. The water smelled putrid, as though lake bottom mud had roiled to the top. The only sound was the swish of water when our debris patch snagged a new piece of rubble. My eyes were adjusting to the darkness. Then a cloud blocked the moon and everything was pitch black. I must have dozed off.

\* \* \* \*

When I woke, streaks of light crisscrossed the sky. Did I hear a boat motor? I froze to listen. The noise stopped.

Voices carried across the water. "You see them?"

"No. I lost them." Was it Rick Crane? I sat up.

"Shine your light on those debris piles, Joe. I'll idle by each one so we can get a good look. Somebody tangled in debris can disappear quickly under the water."

"Here! Here!" I shouted. "Over here!!"

The spotlight danced around us and stopped on my face.

Squinting, I waved frantically. "We're here! Help!"

Sam mumbled something and opened his eyes. A breeze swept over us. I was suddenly cold. Sam was shivering and covered with ants. I saw one crawling toward me and started brushing them off.

"Rick Crane is here, Sam. They're coming for us. Hold on. We're going to be all right."

"I see them!" Joe shouted. "Two people with life jackets." He dimmed the search light.

I closed my eyes to squeeze away the spots and strained through the dim light of dawn, my teeth chattering. Debris from the lake encircled us. A sea of rubbish lay between us and their boat where it idled in the river.

Rick threw out an anchor, cut the motor and called out. "Are you okay? What about your friend?"

"It's Sam Vanderhoven, Rick, from the homeowner's meeting. He needs medical care, but I think he'll be all right. I'm Aggie. Boy, am I glad to see you guys."

"All right, then. We'll figure out a way to get you on board." He turned to Joe. "It's a San Antonio detective and his girlfriend. Nice people."

Forty feet of debris separated us from Rick's boat. How could they get to us? If they drove the boat into the rubble, it would clog the propeller. If they stepped on the brush, they'd fall through into murky water.

In the eerie stillness of the morning, the only sound was light rain failing. They discussed options, their voices carrying clearly across the water.

"If we had wide, flat pieces of plywood," Rick said, "we could float them on top of the debris pile. Maybe I could crawl across them to the victims."

"Okay," Joe said. "Let's see how much we can pull in."

They started catching wide pieces of plywood coming downriver and hauling them into the boat.

I jiggled Sam's good shoulder. His other arm hung at a weird angle. "They're going to come get us, Sam. Are you awake?"

He batted his eyes open and focused on my face. "I can't believe we made it." He looked around. "How'd you get me up here?"

"It wasn't easy."

"Okay. Wake me up when it's time to do something." He closed his eyes.

They must have accumulated enough plywood to span the distance. Rick said, "Let's rig something up and see if I can get this plywood over to them."

Joe took rope coiled on the floor and tied one end to the boat. A few yards down the length of rope, he looped it through a life vest and secured it.

"The vest should keep the rope afloat," Joe said, "so it won't tangle in debris." They estimated the length of rope Rick needed to reach us. Joe tied the rope around Rick and left more rope for us.

"Glad the Marines taught you to tie knots," Rick said. He kicked off his shoes and belt and emptied his pockets. Wearing a green life preserver, he slipped over the side of the boat into black water. "Man! That water is cold!" He kicked awhile, blowing out short breaths, adjusting to the water. "Okay. Hand me a piece of plywood." He lifted and heaved the sheet of plywood as far as he could over the debris toward us. "Give me another one."

Joe handed him one, and he propelled it behind the first one, pushing the first piece closer to us. They repeated the process until they constructed a plywood bridge resting on top of debris from the boat to where we waited.

"Here goes nothing." Rick pulled himself tentatively up onto the first piece of plywood and froze. It held him. He inched across the pieces toward us. His progress was painfully slow.

Joe steadied the boat and lifted the rope so the life vest and rope wouldn't sink in refuse. He called to Rick. "Keep going, buddy. I've got you."

Rick reached us. "Any injuries?"

"Part of a house crashed into Sam," I said. "He thinks he broke his arm and maybe a rib. Take him first. He won't be able to help much. I'm okay. You can come back for me."

"You go first, Aggie," Sam said.

"Don't be silly. You're injured. You need to get in the boat, Sam. I'll be all right." I looked at Rick. "We've been here for hours. Once we were up out of the water, it wasn't so cold. The life jackets helped."

"Those jackets saved you," Rick said, tying the rope around Sam. "Okay, here's what we'll do. I'll lead. You lie on your side, hold the rope with your good arm and crawl sideways over the plywood like a crab. Keep your other arm as still as you can. Got it?"

Sam nodded and got into position. "I love you, Aggie."

"I know. Me, too."

The two men inched their way back. Rick seemed to be keeping them far enough apart so their combined weight wouldn't sink the plywood. They were close to the boat when Sam's leg slid off the flimsy plank. The plywood sheet tilted, tipping him toward the water.

"Hold tight to the rope," Rick yelled. "Lift your leg! Slowly."

If Sam fell off, I didn't think Rick could get him out of the river before they both drowned.

"Hang on, Sam," Joe called. "You're almost there."

The plywood tilted farther, then leveled as Sam dragged his leg back on to the board. Relieved, I started to cry.

"You're good, you're good," Rick said. "Lie there a minute and steady your breathing. When you're ready, we'll head for the boat."

After a few seconds, Sam nodded. Rick began to crawl again, apparently trying to distribute their weight on the makeshift bridge and establish a rhythm to keep them moving toward the boat. Minutes seemed like hours before they reached the side. He and Joe lifted Sam into the boat.

"You're shivering," Joe said. "Here, let's get you into a dry jacket."

Rick climbed in after him, put on a dry jacket and sank against the side of the boat. He took some deep breaths. After several seconds, he climbed back over the side to start the precarious crawl toward me.

As he crept along the improvised road, I started crawling toward him.

"Wait until I get this rope around you," he shouted.

I stopped, the plywood wobbling beneath me. Fortunately, I didn't fall in before he reached me. Since I could use both arms and didn't weigh as much as Sam, Rick led me slightly faster over the thin sheets of wood to the boat. He and Joe lifted me on board.

I crawled over to Sam and held tight to his good side. With his eyes closed, he smiled.

"How can we ever thank you?" I told Rick and Joe. "If I wasn't so dirty and wet, I'd hug you, too."

Their laughter carried across the lake. It was probably the first time they had laughed in hours. A soft rain fell, but the sky grew brighter with daylight. They turned the boat upstream against the current, slowing to listen for voices when they passed a flooded house.

"Anyone in there?" Hearing no answers, they continued upriver. Sam and I leaned against each other, holding hands.

On the side of the lake where I thought we fell in, a man stood alone on the knoll. A truck with a boat trailer was parked hear him.

The man shouted to Rick and Joe. "Go on to the I-10 slip. I'll meet you there with your truck, and we'll get your boat out."

"That's Dave Kelly," Rick said. "He kept my truck from going over the dam."

Rick steered the eighteen-footer upriver through floating debris. The Mercury motor made a grinding sound. He said to Joe in a low voice, "I hope this engine lasts long enough to get us to I-10." Joe nodded.

On either side of the ramp under I-10, firemen in parkas and rubber boots held devices like long-handled pitchforks and used them to shove tree limbs and refuse off the concrete ramp. Rick idled the boat, waiting for the ramp and the approach to clear.

When Rick waved, Dave Kelly jumped into the cab to maneuver Rick's truck and trailer backwards down the ramp into shallow water. Rick drove the boat straight onto the trailer, and two firemen secured the connection. Rick and Joe clambered over the side and jumped into the cab with Dave. Dave pulled the boat, with us in it, up the slope through slippery mud and continued up the paved road to the I-10 overpass.

We made it.

To sighs of relief and clapping, the men got us out and we stood by the boat, dripping, covered in mud, and shaky with exhaustion.

Rick pointed to us. "I need to take them to Guadalupe County Hospital. Sam has a broken arm."

"Let's get the passengers into your cab," Dave said to Rick. "That's my truck over there. We can trailer your boat behind my truck." He turned to Joe. "Can you come with me and direct me to your boat storage?"

"You bet," Joe said. "My truck is at the boat barn." He turned to Rick. "If we were cats," he said, "we just used up eight of our nine lives."

# THIRTEEN

As we headed to the hospital, Sam was so glad we made it, his broken arm didn't seem to bother him.

"How are the ant bites?" I asked.

"I have lots of welts, but they stopped itching."

Rick pulled up to the Emergency Room and went in to tell them about us. Orderlies came out with wheel chairs and blankets and rolled us into changing rooms off the ER. I stripped off my wet clothes and shivered, remembering how cold it was in the lake. What I wouldn't give for a hot bath and shampoo. I looked around for a shower. No such luck.

I could easily have lost Sam. If I hadn't been so eager to have some time alone with him, he might not have gone to the lake at all. He might have seen the weather forecast and picked another weekend to investigate the theft of Chuck's boat.

I dried myself with a towel and roughed up my hair to shake out debris. If I'd gone with Alice and insisted that Sam go with us, we would have been safe. By going with Jess in the patrol car, we put ourselves in greater danger.

And there was Grace. If I'd told her we were going, she could have been watching the weather and called to warn us. She could have called her step-grandson or a friend and been safely out of her house before it flooded. I'd let down the people I loved. So eager to please myself, I forgot about everyone else. After a tragedy, did everyone look back with regrets?

My limbs still felt stiff from the cold water. The orderly came in to help me into hospital scrubs. She wrapped a blanket around me and pushed me back to the ER to wait. Rick was there. Another orderly wheeled Sam in, wrapped in a blanket.

"Did they put something on your ant bites?

"Most of them."

"How's your arm?"

"It's numb from the cold. As long as I don't move it, it's okay."

Rick handed us clipboards with hospital forms. When we finished filling them in, he took them to the desk and returned.

"You don't need to stay, Rick," I said.

"You don't have a place to stay, do you?"

"We can get a cab and find a motel," Sam said.

"With no community shelter for flood victims, motels might be filling pretty fast. When we're through here, I'll take you to find one."

"You keep on saving us, Rick," I said.

"It's my job. Sam knows about that."

Sam nodded. "Thanks, buddy."

"Rick," I said, "I've been thinking about everything that happened. Early Saturday morning, we saw two people across the lake from Chuck's house arguing on the dock. It was dark and starting to thunder, and they were wearing hooded raincoats, so we couldn't identify them or hear what they said. A few minutes later, when lightning illuminated the dock, they had disappeared. Did you rescue anyone from that house?"

"We launched at the end of Turtle Lane Saturday," he said. "We plucked a couple people off roofs over there, but I don't remember picking up two people in raincoats. Most of the people we picked up were downriver, closer to the dam. You don't know who they were?"

"No."

A nurse called from the front of the room. "Sam Vander-hoven."

I gave his good hand a squeeze. "Looks like you're going to get your arm set."

Sam came out a half-hour later with a white pla
from his wrist, over his elbow, to midway up his upp
"If I have transportation, they say I can leave."

Rick nodded. "I'll tell them I'm your ride."

"Thanks, Rick."

"Does it hurt?" I asked.

"No. And my ribs aren't broken, just bruised. That's why they took me so fast. They thought I might have internal injuries from broken ribs. They gave me a shot of something they said will last until tomorrow." He gave me a goofy grin.

They left us in scrubs with blankets and handed us our wet clothes in plastic bags. Orderlies wheeled us to Rick's truck and helped us into the cab. A light rain still fell.

"I think my car is pretty near 90A," Sam said. "Can you swing by there? My left arm was broken, but I can drive with my right. Or Aggie can drive."

"Sure."

Rick drove back to Highway 90. Sam's car stood in the middle of a muddy field between 90 and I-10.

"That car's not going anywhere," Rick said. "You're stuck in that field until the ground dries. The rain's letting up. If it stops, maybe it will dry out enough tomorrow for you to get your car out. Let's go over toward I-10 and find you a place to stay."

Although he didn't realize it, Sam was in no condition to drive. Rick drove farther away from Lake Placid. How many residents had survived? Did Alice Stapleton make it to her friend's house? Did Chuck still have a lake house? The people we saw on the dock could have been with us in the Army vehicle. Or inside another truck. Or in the river. Chills rippled over me. They might never be found.

Rick turned on Highway 123 and switched on the radio. Seguin, New Braunfels, San Marcos, and San Antonio were flooded. DPS had closed highway access to sections of Highway 90 and IH-35 and told people to stay put. No one could get to San Antonio.

*stic cast
r arm.*

`cono-Taj and pulled into the parking lot.
nbled toward the entrance.

urvive that flood," Rick said.

great job. Thanks."

ng," he said. "I think we picked up thir-

us." I smiled.

unced back to the car, grinning. "We got the last
n the second floor."

We thanked Rick again. "And tell Joe how grateful we
are." With their skill and bravery, he and Joe saved many
lives. Sam grasped his hand. I hugged him.

# FOURTEEN

Swathed in blankets and reeking of river mud, we walked into the lobby. Not wanting to smell ourselves in the tiny elevator, we took the stairs to the second floor. The room with two double beds was no palace, but it was clean and dry.

I extracted my bagged phone from the waistband of my scrubs. It was out of battery power and slightly damp. I headed for the bathroom and turned on the shower. Two drops dripped from the spigot.

I dressed and returned to the bedroom. "No water."

"I saw bottled water in the lobby along with buckets. I forgot to tell you. They said at the desk we're supposed to use pool water for baths and flushing. At least we have electricity."

I went to our small balcony and peered down at the swimming pool. Despite a light rain, three people were hauling buckets of pool water to their rooms. "I better go get some. I'll ask the desk for a phone charger."

"I'm going to lie on the floor for a second. I'm too dirty to get on the bed. I'll come down later and help you haul water."

I was dirty and sticky but so glad to be alive, I didn't feel tired. Sam must be extra weary from the stress of responsibility and the trauma of a broken arm.

After borrowing a phone charger and retrieving a bucket from the front desk, I made my way to the pool. A woman stood by the edge, efficiently lowering her bucket into the pool.

"You look like you've done this before," I said.

"Three times, so far. Flushing and bathing takes a lot of water. Connie Knott. I'm in 204."

"Aggie Mundeen. My boyfriend Sam and I are in 206. He said we got the last room."

"I don't doubt it. You'd think towns with rivers nearby would have someplace for people to gather in an emergency." She put one bucket down and started filling another.

"What about the hospital?" I asked.

"They're busy taking care of the injured. They can't let people use it for shelter. Our nursing home wasn't flooded, thank goodness, but the poor souls can't go anywhere. Many of their family members can't get to them."

"You work at a nursing home?"

"I'm administrator of Pecan Paradise. I rented a room here early on, thinking if my neighborhood flooded, I needed to be prepared. I live upstream, near Lake Placid, so my house has water damage. But when the water supply was interrupted in Seguin, the rain was a blessing to our nursing home. We gathered water in plastic barrels and use them to flush toilets and for cleaning."

"If only everybody were as well prepared."

"Well, my residents depend on me providing. Do you live on the lake?"

"We were taking care of a friend's house at Lake Placid. We got out when the water started rising, but I bet his house is a mess. I'll have to check on it when I can. I feel like I ought to help clean it up.

"Maybe I can help."

"It'll be nasty work. Do you need supplies for the nursing home?"

"Before the rain started," she said, "I went to Walmart and bought all the bottled water I could. I checked on my residents a couple times today. My assistant is spending the night. I don't know what I'd do without her."

"Do they have enough food?"

"We maintain supplies for a one-month rotation of meals, so there's no shortage of food. I'll have to find fresh produce, though."

I started filling my bucket. "How much water was in your home?"

"About a foot."

I shook my head.

"It's mostly drained off, but there's a lot of clean-up to do before I can move back. I'll have to run the nursing home from here."

"How awful. I'm so sorry."

"Hey, I'm lucky compared to a lot of people. I'm alive with a job, a car, a home that will dry out and people I can help."

I liked her attitude.

"There's no place you can stay at the nursing home?"

"I have a nice office and my own private bath, but it's really better for me not to live there 24/7. Instead of the administrator, I'd become the house mother."

"I see what you mean. Want me to help you buy supplies tomorrow?"

"That would be great." She picked up her buckets. "Shall I knock on your door about nine?"

"Perfect. I'll be ready." She walked away. If Sam's car wouldn't start, he could help, too. I concentrated on filling my bucket with swimming pool water.

A young woman appeared at the pool with a boy about four. She abandoned her bucket to chase him around the pool so he wouldn't jump in.

"Looks like you're busy. I'll fill it for you." I dipped her bucket.

"Thank you," she said. "He's been confined in our room, and he's ready to run. I don't know how I'm going to entertain him until we can go home."

I filled her bucket and took it to her. She gripped her son's hand, grabbed the bucket with the other and walked toward the lobby. "This bath is going to be interesting."

A tragedy affected so many people.

Sam appeared beside me with a bucket. "Good thing this is a big pool. If my car doesn't start, we may be here a while."

"I met a lady who might drive you to your car. Connie Knott. She's director of Pecan Paradise Nursing Home, but she's staying here while her house dries out. I'm going to help her shop tomorrow. If your car doesn't start, you can help, too. There's a young woman with a four-year-old who might also need help."

Sam staggered and almost dropped the bucket. He looked pale and drawn.

"Want me to take up your bucket?" I asked, guilty over suggesting another chore.

He took a couple of deep breaths. "No. I can get it." He picked up his bucket and trudged toward the stairs.

When I got upstairs, I heard him floundering in the shower. "Need help?" I called. It's not easy to bathe with one arm.

"I've got it."

He eventually came out of the bathroom in hospital scrubs with the blanket wrapped around him and his hair sticking up in points. His cast looked pretty dry. I plugged in my phone.

"I got our clothes out of the plastic bags," he said. "They smell terrible." He picked up my bucket and hauled it to the bathroom. "I have water left in my bucket if you need it. I'll see what I can get on the news."

I went to the bathroom, hopped into the shower, scrubbed with soap and rinsed with pool water, hoping the chlorine wouldn't make me itch. I dried myself and put the scrubs back on. Our muddy clothes smelled so bad I washed them in pool water before I hung them on the bathroom bar to dry. When I came out, Sam was under the sheets, leaning against the headboard, eyes glued to television.

"Would you lower the volume? I want to try to call Grace."

Miraculously, my damp phone sprang to life. I let it ring and ring. No answer. Her neighbor on the other side was vacationing in the northeast. I didn't know how to find her step-grandson. "Can you call headquarters and have them send someone to her house?"

"I'm sure SAPD is swamped helping flood victims. If I can get in tomorrow, I'll check on her."

We dozed off with the television on and woke up starving. "They have bottled water downstairs and frozen dinners. I'll see what I can get." He came out of the bathroom dressed in his clothes, with a pinched expression. "My clothes are damp and smell like chlorine."

"I washed them in pool water. I thought it smelled better than lake mud."

"I reek," he said with a sniff. "I hope they let me stay in the lobby long enough to buy food."

When he came back, he went straight to the bathroom, hung up his clothes and donned scrubs again. We heated the dinners in the room's microwave and scarfed them down watching the news. Sam reeked of chlorine, but I ignored it.

"Do you think Chuck's house is ruined?" I asked.

"Hard to tell."

"We'll have to assess the damage," I said.

"When we can. Police will close off the area. There'll be danger from debris and looters. Maybe in a day or two, they'll let people in."

"If it's salvageable, we could help clean it up."

He sighed. "We'll see."

When we finished eating, he turned down the volume. Full but exhausted, we fell asleep with lights from the screen flickering across the room.

\* \* \* \* \*

I woke slowly. Was that the sound of a familiar voice? I sat up. Did it come from the television? I blinked at the fluorescent screen. The volume was off. I could swear I heard Grace's voice.

I tiptoed to the set, turned it off and stood by the door to the balcony. The rain had eased, so I slipped outside and closed the door. I heard Grace's voice as clearly as if she were standing next to me.

*"You've had quite a weekend, haven't you, Aggie? Me, too. I was totally absorbed tiling a table when you'll-never-guess-who walked in."*

I waited.

*"Ray Peters."*

My jaw dropped. Ray was her beloved third husband. He died from metastatic cancer a year ago.

*"I always knew we'd see each other again."*

My heart skipped. Where was she? Was Grace…?

*"He came over and started talking, just like we never missed a beat. He'd been waiting for me to settle in before he came. Now that I established my usual routine, he thought it was time to pick up where we were."*

"Did he look the same? Could you touch him?"

*"Exactly the same. Of course I touched him. We hugged. It felt like two halves of a whole getting back together."*

"Are there other people around?"

*"I haven't seen any, but he said I'd start seeing people I knew. He wanted to be first."*

"Were you…? Is your house… Was it flooded?"

*"Yes. It's a mess. Yours too, I'm afraid. Yours will probably take longer to fix. I'm so glad you made it through. That flood was incredible! I wouldn't worry about your house. Things will work out. They always do. And a lot of people where you are need help."*

"Grace, where are you? Are you hurt?" She didn't sound hurt. In fact, she sounded happy. "Where are you? I can't get home now, but I need to find you."

She didn't answer. I waited. I called her name a couple times. Nothing. Had the shock of the flood made me crazy?

Traumatic events affected people differently. Maybe I imagined her voice to reassure me that if Sam or I had died in the flood, it wouldn't be the last time we'd see each other.

I tiptoed into the bedroom, not sure what I would find. Sam, uttering an occasional snore, slept peacefully.

# FIFTEEN

We woke early, put on dry clothes and went downstairs to forage. The menu was bottled water and frozen breakfast tacos. Other refugees smelled worse than we did, but some people were giving us funny looks, so we went upstairs to eat. We filled more buckets with pool water and called Grace and SAPD. I got no answer. Sam connected with dispatch and said he had his arm in a cast but could drive and would be there as soon as his car cooperated.

I didn't mention my nocturnal conversation with Grace. He'd suffered enough trauma. I didn't want him to worry about my sanity.

Promptly at nine, there was a knock on the door. Connie Knott stood there with a smile. I introduced Sam, and he asked if she had time to take him to his car near I-10.

"Sure. Glad to. It's just down the road."

I waited in her car while Sam went to check his soggy vehicle. On the third try, the engine turned over and caught. The car wasn't that far from the highway, and he managed to get onto the access road without getting stuck in the mud. We pulled up beside him.

"Thanks, Connie," he said. "I'm headed to SA. DPS will tell me the best route. I can't wait to get a bath and fresh clothes." He pulled his wallet out of the glove compartment. "Here, Aggie, take this credit card. I'll call the company and tell them you can sign on it."

"That's wonderful, Sam. I think my purse is still in the lake house. Are you sure you can drive with one arm?"

"No problem."

"Okay. I'll go with Connie to pick up supplies, then head to the nursing home."

He looked at Connie. "You two will be safe?"

She nodded. He smiled and pulled away.

"Nice to have a man who cares about you."

"He's a San Antonio detective. I think it's part of his DNA"

She smiled.

At the store, I selected clothes and bought a few personal hygiene items. For Connie's residents, we got bottled water, vegetables, fruit, milk, orange juice, and cheese. On the way to the nursing home, she told me about Pecan Paradise.

"It's a really nice facility with a hundred-forty-five beds. Fortunately, we have enough bed and bath supplies to keep everyone clean. But all the laundry has to be transported to a laundromat twenty miles away. That's a huge undertaking."

"I can imagine."

She shrugged. "It's a small town, so services are limited. And Pecan Paradise is filling up. With the new people who came in after the flood, we're almost to capacity. Family members brought them in because they were traumatized."

"Poor things! It must have been a horrible experience for them."

"Yes. One woman brought her sister in yesterday on their doctor's recommendation. The patient won't talk or eat. Her sister hopes she can rest and recover at our home. If not, the doctor will consider other options. Don't mention this to anyone. She's a long-time lake resident: Verna Weller."

"Verna's there? I met her and Maxwell and her sister at a homeowner's meeting the night before the flood. They lived across the lake from the cottage where Sam and I stayed. I'm so glad she escaped. That whole area was under water. Verna had been in a flood before and was afraid of living on the lake. Some guy named Sledge kept trying to get the Wellers to sell him their house or let him build it up on stilts."

"Garner Sledge?" she said with a dry laugh. "Everybody knows Garner."

"How did he fare?"

"Fine, I guess. He's probably scouting for cheap property. But Max Weller is missing."

"No!" I thought about the people on the dock. Were they the Wellers? Had Max fallen into the water and Verna been rescued? I decided not to tell Connie what I saw. It might not have been them.

"Are the people at Pecan Paradise aware of the flood?" I asked.

"Most of them are. They're glued to the television, and many have family in the area. Some are stunned and in shock from having lost all the memorabilia from their family homes. They or their children are left with nothing but mud-filled shells. The need for temporary housing is overwhelming."

We reached the nursing home and unloaded enough supplies for a M.A.S.H. unit. After I helped her put away groceries, she said she needed to check on the occupants. First, she was going to bathe and put on clean clothes.

"Is there a place I can bathe and change?" I asked.

She pointed to an empty room and bath down the hall. "I'll get you some rainwater to wash in, and then I'll meet you back in the kitchen."

I ran to the room with my Walmart bag. Once I was clean and in fresh clothes, I felt like a new woman.

I found Connie back in the kitchen. "I'm not crazy about the fashion," I said, indicating my clothes, "but I know I smell better. Is there anything I can do?"

"Not really. You've helped already. It'll take me about an hour to check on the residents. I need to verify we have enough medical supplies and make sure my assistant Tanya knows times and dosages for everybody."

"What room is Verna in? I might peep in. If she's awake, I'll just say 'hello' and tell her I'm glad she's here. Is that okay?"

"Yes, but you might be disappointed. I doubt she'll recognize you."

Not knowing what to expect, I tiptoed into Verna's room. She sat straight up in bed with her hands folded, looking directly ahead with a blank stare. Her body looked tense, expectant, as if she was gearing up for bad news or anticipating a blow. I leaned into her line of vision with a smile on my face. She blinked, but her expression didn't change.

"I'm glad to see you again after the homeowner's meeting," I said. No response. "It was a terrible flood. But we made it, didn't we?" No response. "Well, I'll see you later then." I backed out of the room.

I checked the wall clock. Connie must be busy visiting occupants, so I decided to go to the community television lounge I passed on the way to Verna's room. I peeked in. Residents engaged in lively conversation sat at card tables playing games. At the other end of the room, people lounged in a semi-circle of sofas and chairs to watch TV footage of the flood. I slipped into the nearest chair.

Before I settled, the man at the end of the adjacent sofa leaned toward me. "You new here?"

"No," I smiled. "Just visiting."

He nodded, his eyebrows peaking into a wrinkled forehead. "I thought you were too young. We love visitors. Takes our mind off families and friends wiped out by the dang flood. But everybody will get back to normal. They always do."

"It was awful. We were staying in a friend's house. We left in time, but I'm afraid his house is ruined." I offered my hand. "Aggie Mundeen."

"Tucker Bastrop. Pleased to meet you. You have family here?"

"No. I came to help Connie unload groceries."

"Connie's a love."

"Yes, she is."

While Tucker recounted tales about people who were flooded, the woman to his right kept tilting forward, straining to see around him. When he ran out of flood stories and took a breath, she poked him and thrust herself forward.

He jumped. "I'm sorry, Lizzie." He leaned back so she and I could see each other. "This is Lizzie Fallon. Her daughter lives in the Panhandle and brings Lizzie's grandkids to visit. She's my Scrabble partner."

"Hello, Aggie. I heard your name. We'd be in a hot Scrabble match today if those people hadn't hogged all the tables." She scowled.

"I love Scrabble. Maybe we can play next time I come. Connie might have another game table stored somewhere. She's probably ready to run errands now, but I'll ask her."

Smiles lit their faces. I loved talking with enthusiastic people.

I walked back to the lobby and plopped into a comfy chair to call Sam, but visiting with Tucker and Lizzie, I'd lost track of time. Before the call connected, Connie marched in.

"Okay. Everything's good here. I'll help you clean up at Lake Placid, but I think we're too clean to slog through mud today. Can we wait until tomorrow? I'm ready to put my feet up."

"Sure. I wasn't even sure you had time to help me. That's wonderful!" I smiled in relief. "By the way, poor Verna seems so traumatized. I'd like to learn more about how a disaster like this affects people. If the Seguin Public Library is open, would you mind dropping me off there on your way to the motel? I can get a cab home."

"A cab? We don't even have good bus service. The library should be open. It's quite far from the lake. I'll pick you up when you're through. Just call me."

"You'll hate having to get out again."

"No trouble. Econo-Taj will be there when I get back."

Nursing home residents were really lucky to have Connie. She was a born caregiver.

Before I visited Verna again, if I could learn more about the emotional effects of living through a disaster, I might be able to help her. When Connie dropped me at the library, I walked to the information desk and asked to use the computers. The girl eyeballed me like I had presented her with a warrant for Search and Seizure.

"We just received new computers," she said. "We've barely used them ourselves."

I appraised the computer area. "I've used machines just like those at University of the Holy Trinity in San Antonio. My computer at home is similar. I use it all the time."

She rose slowly from her desk, one fish eye on me and the other on her beloved machines. She approached the computer area at a snail's pace, glancing left and right for a senior librarian to bail her out. She apparently wasn't ready to subject her library's new toys to public use.

I floated down in front of a machine. "Beautiful," I purred. "I'll handle it with great care." I powered it up, pressing keys ever so gently, to access the internet.

My actions froze her to the spot. Finally, she took a deep, cleansing breath. Satisfied that I could be trusted to not incapacitate her machine, she reluctantly left us alone.

I found an article on how trauma affects the brain. "Trauma disrupts the stress-hormone system and plays havoc with the entire nervous system, which prevents people from processing and integrating traumatic memories into conscious mental frameworks."

I supposed that's why Verna appeared inanimate but tense, like she was about to jump out of her skin. She was terrified, without being able to process what happened.

"Flood trauma can have great impact on a person's psychosocial needs and mental health," I read. "The severity and length of their mental distress depend largely on the extent of their loss and how much emotional support they had before and after the event."

Verna had lost everything. Their home was unquestionably obliterated. And Max wasn't around to offer support. I hoped he survived and would appear and calmly walk through her door. Thank goodness Verna had Gwen. My heart ached over what Grace might have endured alone.

I learned other salient facts about flood victims, printed them out to study later, and guiltily called Connie to pick me up. When we got back to Econo-Taj, I knew I'd better haul water up from the pool before I crashed. I deposited two buckets in the bathroom and collapsed on the bed to call Sam.

# SIXTEEN

I dialed Sam's number. "Did you find Grace?"

"I'm afraid not, Aggie. When we went to her house, the front door was open. We found her shoes by the door, as though she put on another pair before she went out. There was no umbrella in the stand. The entry hall and part of the living room were soaked. Her purse and keys were on the hall table, and her car was in the garage. There was no evidence of foul play."

"She kept rubber boots by the umbrella stand to use for yard work or if it was raining." I rested my head in my hand. "Why would she go outside in a storm?"

"You told me how much she loves Boffo. Maybe he tore down the street and she tried to catch him. We called the hospitals, too. So far, nothing."

My heart sank. I didn't make sense for her to chase Boffo out into the rain. She could have called to him. He would eventually come back. I tried to think of another reason why she was missing, but I couldn't come up with anything.

"Her neighbor on the other side is out of town, but you could leave a note under the door and ask him to let you know when Grace comes back," I said.

"I'll do that."

"There was no sign of Boffo?"

"No."

Grace wouldn't go very far without Boffo. I hoped they were somewhere together, confused and traumatized perhaps, but alive. Hearing her voice must have been wishful thinking on my part.

"We got into your house, too. I'm afraid it's worse than hers. A couple windows were broken by tree limbs. I called a repair man to replace the windows, but the floors are ruined and probably all the appliances—everything is soaked a couple feet up from the floor. It will be expensive to restore."

My heart was a stone. "Thank you for looking for Grace and checking our houses." I tried to be positive. "I'm lucky to have a place to stay. The motel is giving us a weekly rate. Should I file a missing person report?"

"You can file one, but SAPD requires a family member or guardian to file an official report. She could have been picked up by somebody, be disoriented, have amnesia. Sometimes people call hospitals instead of police. Right now, things are in turmoil around here. Give me all the data about her you know, and I'll put it on this form. Tomorrow, I'll have a patrolman search her house for her step-grandson's name and address."

I sighed. "Thank you, Sam. I bet you have a pile of other work to do. How's your arm?"

"It's okay. It throbs once in a while, but Advil takes care of it. They have me doing a lot of paperwork and riding around with other officers. I do need to stay in town and help out. They've spent the last two days helping flood victims, and more people need help."

"I'm fine at the motel. When I helped Connie stock up for the nursing home, I even bought clean clothes. I'll help her at the home tomorrow, and she's glad to take me wherever I need to go. She's going to take me to the lake house to see its condition and will take pictures for Chuck's insurance company."

"That's great. I'll let him know."

"By the way, Verna Weller is at the nursing home. Her sister Gwen brought her in for care until she gets back to normal. I stepped into her room for a minute. I think she's in shock from the flood. Max Weller is apparently missing."

Sam sighed. "I wasn't going to tell you yet, but since you know he's missing... police found his body in the lake early Sunday morning."

"Oh, no. Poor Max. Poor Verna."

"Jess Perez called me. Max looked like he drowned, but he had a gash on the back of his head, and they think that's what killed him. They don't know if debris hit him in the water or if somebody hit him before he fell in. They sent him to San Antonio for autopsy."

"Verna's already in shock. How can she withstand this?"

"That's why SAPD didn't contact her. With the manner of his death questionable, the consensus was to wait until we had the facts before questioning Verna and Gwen. We might need a doctor present. Far as we can determine, Verna and Max have no family other than Gwen."

"Maybe Verna and Max were arguing on the dock," I said. "But why would she hit him? She would have been too petrified of the swirling water to think about hitting Max."

"From what we heard at the homeowners' meeting, I doubt they'd be out on the dock at all. If they were, and Max fell in, Verna could have panicked, run into the house, and someone rescued her," he said.

"She could be in shock from what she saw. Or in denial."

"Or consumed with guilt," he said. "I called Rick Crane to see what he knows about Max. He said the guy was fearless, loved the lake, lived on the edge and was probably out fishing before the flood came, enjoying the elements. He drank a lot, too."

"And took barbiturates. Maybe he took too many. I was planning to visit Verna tomorrow. Maybe a kind voice will help bring her back. I won't mention Max."

"That sounds good. Let me know how she is and how the house looks so I can let Chuck know. I'll get caught up here. When things settle down, I'll come back to the lake and help."

"You're great, Sam."

"I know." He hung up.

I thought about what he said. The odds were that Max drowned. He had lived on the lake forever and preferred fishing to socializing. Who could want him dead? Garner Sledge had designs on their house, but why kill Max in a storm, with the water rising? If he wanted the property, all he had to do was wait until later, canvas the neighborhood for devastation and approach distressed owners with low-ball offers.

Poor Verna and Max. I wondered if Alice knew what had happened to them. Probably not. Everything happened so fast.

# SEVENTEEN

"After we stock the shelves at Pecan Paradise, this will be a good day to go to Lake Placid," Connie said. "But to get near the house and do anything, we need high-topped rubber boots, heavy-duty work gloves, and shovels."

We found everything we needed and added a few staples, fresh produce and more cheese for the residents. When I helped Connie put away groceries, the smell of fresh cheddar made my stomach rumble. I was getting really tired of Econo-Taj's frozen dinners, but trekking to a restaurant to eat would take more energy than we had. When we put up fresh peaches, bananas, and tomatoes, I whiffed each one before I tucked it away. I didn't want to pilfer food from nursing home residents, but if I didn't eat fruit and salad pretty soon, I'd die of scurvy.

A few gray heads popped into the kitchen while we were stashing goodies. Residents' eyes darted between treasure extracted from grocery bags to the inside of the refrigerators.

"Okay, that's done." Connie folded the last bag. "I'll go see how everyone's doing." The peepers' heads disappeared. I could hear them scurrying down the hall to be in their rooms for Connie's visit.

"It is okay if I visit Verna?"

"Sure."

As I neared Verna's room, her sister stepped into the hall and closed the door behind her.

"Hello, Gwen. Sam and I met you with Verna and Max at the Lake Placid homeowners' meeting. Aggie Mundeen."

She nodded, looking drawn and ten years older. "I remember. It seems like a lifetime ago."

"I'm so sorry they lost their home. What a terrible tragedy."

"It's hard to comprehend. Police blocked the entry to Pecan Cove. They say mud from the lake is so high on the road, we'd get stuck. So we can't even go see if there's anything left." She looked down and shook her head. "I don't think Verna could stand seeing it anyway. They tell me she wakes up screaming. She must have terrible nightmares. When I come during the day, she's jumpy and tense, like she anticipates something horrible."

"Didn't she live through another flood?"

She nodded. "They say previous trauma makes PTSD even worse."

The term PTSD popped up in my research, but I hadn't heard Gwen use the term to describe her sister's condition. Maybe as a school nurse, she was familiar with the term. Or perhaps she had done some research of her own.

"It's good you brought her here to recuperate." I paused. "I'm so sorry to hear your brother-in-law is missing."

She nodded. Apparently, that was all local police told her. "He loves the water. Likes it even better under an overcast sky with the wind blowing. It's so typical of him to go out on the lake late Friday or Saturday with the weather changing. And then to get caught in the storm."

"No one predicted this much rain and flooding."

"No. They said after the lakes flooded upstream, the rainstorm stalled over our area. I've never seen water rise like that."

"Were you with Verna when the flood started?"

"I was on my way there and got stopped at the entrance. I had to park and watch from the bridge. Boats and debris were hurling downriver and people were driving boats upstream against the current trying to dodge them."

"You didn't see Max in his boat?"

"No." Her eyes filled.

"I'm sorry… I shouldn't have…" I patted her hand. "I'm so sorry."

"It's all right. I just keep trying to picture where he was when the storm hit. He was probably out in that darn boat. He's obsessive about it. If he weren't so bullheaded, he might be here with Verna right now."

"I don't know what she'd do without you, Gwen. You must be exhausted. Your house in town wasn't damaged? Can you rest there?"

"My house is high and dry, thank goodness. But I'm still the school nurse, so I have to go there every day."

She looked away, as if she was remembering the past. "Verna used to be right next door when she was married to Bob."

"That was a happy time?"

Her eyes wet, she produced a weak smile. "Yes."

"If you think it's all right, I'll visit her a minute."

"Move slowly and quietly. She's easily startled." She let out a sigh. "My body feels odd. I haven't been eating properly."

"You've got to take care of yourself, Gwen." Verna's rehabilitation would be totally on her shoulders.

"I do need to be careful. I've been ignoring the signs." She trudged down the corridor with slumped shoulders.

I opened the door to Verna's room and moved cautiously in, speaking in a soft, encouraging voice.

"Verna, it's Aggie. I just saw Gwen in the hall. Is it all right if I come in for a minute?"

She tensed, sat straighter, drew her arms tight to her sides and stared straight ahead.

I moved into her line of vision. "Are you feeling any better? This is such a lovely room. You're quite safe here with everyone caring for you. I'm so glad Gwen is here to help you." She twitched, then turned her head toward the window and gazed through it with unseeing eyes.

Her twitch probably meant she didn't feel safe. Who would after what happened? One symptom of PTSD trauma was feeling constantly on guard. It would take a long time before she felt safe. And poor Gwen would have to deal with everything. What a load. She didn't seem well herself.

Feeling helpless, I spoke in a soothing voice. "I'm sure each day will be better, Verna." I was a lousy liar. I didn't think things would be better for a long time. I eased backward and shuffled down the hall toward the lobby. Hearing laughter in the lounge, I peered in.

Three tables of people played games. One foursome played Bridge, which I enjoyed, and the Scrabble table had three people. I recognized Lizzie and Tucker and walked over. "Need a fourth?" I said.

"You bet."

After an hour of laughing and good companionship, I strolled to the lobby to wait for Connie. She bustled in, looking content.

"Tanya distributed meds, and everybody's full of lunch and comfortable," she said. "They'll be napping. How is Verna?"

"Jumpy, but okay. Her sister Gwen didn't look like she felt well."

"She's diabetic. She mentioned it to the nurse who comes by to check our residents. Gwen probably needs to evaluate her diet and insulin schedule. She'll get herself back on track." She held up a sheet of paper. "A couple of our residents have family members living on Lake Placid. Tanya gave me their names, so we can check on them. We can grab a hamburger on the way." I liked being part of Connie's helper brigade. "First, you and I need to get tetanus shots at the hospital."

"A shot? Why do we need to do that?" I said. "We're just going to slosh around in mud."

"Exactly. You don't know what's buried in there. Could be rusty objects, sharp pieces from boats, lawn chairs, houses. We can't afford to step on something. If we get a cut or puncture wound, bacteria can get in and cause lockjaw. Muscle spasms in your face and mouth are so bad you can't even open your mouth. That's the most common symptom."

That sounded horrible. I wouldn't be able to eat. Or talk.

"You can get spasms in your abdomen, stomach, or extremities, too. In thirty percent of cases, lockjaw can be fatal."

"Okay, okay. I'm convinced." We drove in silence to the hospital. I *hated* shots.

# EIGHTEEN

Connie pulled into Guadalupe Regional Medical Center near the Emergency Room. I trudged behind her into the packed waiting room. From the smell of lake-bottom mud, I suspected some people were there for minor problems and needed a safe place to regroup until they could figure out their next move.

We saw the sign: "Tetanus Vaccines." Connie and I were told to fill out a lengthy medical questionnaire and join the line of people waiting. The line moved pretty fast. I told her to go first. I wanted to see her expression when she came out. If she looked distressed, I'd skirt out of line and take my chances at Lake Placid.

"Next."

When Connie went into the cubicle, the nurse pulled the curtain across behind her, which made the whole operation look nefarious. I waited at least five minutes. My heart rate increased until I could actually hear it beating. I sometimes experienced strange reactions to shots but hated to be a wimp.

The nurse swished back the curtain and Connie came out. "Nothing to it."

I swallowed and entered the cubicle. I noted the cot in the room, sat in the chair nearest to it and tried to ignore the rustle of the curtain closing behind me.

"How are we today?" said a nurse as she entered.

I didn't know how "we" were, but I was scared spitless. If people could die from lockjaw, what would the injection do? The nurse cleaned off my upper arm with wet cotton. I felt lightheaded.

"Have you heard of a vasovagal reaction?" I said weakly, attempting to explain how I felt.

She frowned over her glasses. "Of course," she said. "But not for a silly shot."

My field of vision narrowed. Her brows knit together like caterpillar asps. I felt clammy and cold. Wham. She let me have it. I grabbed her arm, hoping to remain upright.

"Oh, for Pete's sake." She dragged me from the chair, lugged my limp body to the cot, lay me down and shoved a pillow under my knees. I lay motionless, wondering if the pain would set in before my jaw locked.

She ripped open the curtain. "Anybody here with Agatha Mundeen?" she barked.

I opened my eyes and blinked up at Connie's concerned face.

"What's wrong?" she asked Nurse Asp.

"Your friend had a vasovagal reaction to the injection. Can you believe it? You'll have to wait here until she feels normal. God knows how long it will slow down our tetanus line."

Connie pulled up a chair. "How do you feel?"

I took a deep breath and my vision cleared. "Better. What happened?"

"Your emotion activated your vagal nerves, your heart rate slowed, your blood pressure dropped and you felt faint. I've learned a lot running a nursing home."

A man who looked about twelve came over and introduced himself as the Emergency Room Physician. "I'm Dr. Billups," he said. "How do you feel?"

"Better." The shot thing was over, and I could still talk. I moved my jaw side to side.

"We think you had a vasovagal response to having the injection. Has this happened before?"

"A couple times." It happened almost every time I got shots or saw blood. I hated to admit it. Especially with Nurse Asp looming.

"Do you have any heart or blood pressure problems?"

I shook my head. He put his stethoscope on my chest and had me take deep breaths. Then he held my wrist to take my pulse. "Everything seems normal. You should wait here twenty minutes, then get up slowly. If you have no further problems, you're free to leave."

"Thank you, Doctor."

He smiled and left.

Asp uttered a disgusted sigh and yanked back the curtain to explain the delay to people waiting.

I felt really stupid. "I'm sorry, Connie."

"No problem. It happens to one in four people. I'm the same way about snakes."

I closed my eyes, grateful for Connie, for Sam, for surviving the flood, for shots that prevented lockjaw and for baby-faced physicians who appeared competent. For Nurse Asp, not so much. Guess I should have warned her more emphatically.

When my symptoms passed, I sat up slowly, feeling silly. Chin up, I walked past the line of staring, disgruntled people. "Nobody's perfect," I said.

We continued outside to Connie's car and headed for Lake Placid.

# NINETEEN

When we pulled up to the Lake Placid subdivision entrance, Police Officer Jesse Perez came to the car.

"Hello, Jess," I said. "I hope you've had a chance to eat and get some sleep."

"Hello, Miss Aggie. We had time for a nap or two, but we've got a real mess here. There's so much destruction, it looks like a war zone. Nobody can go in except residents."

"This is Connie Knott, Director at Pecan Paradise Nursing Home. A couple of her residents asked her to check on relatives who live here."

"I have a list of homeowners," he said. Connie handed him her names.

"All these people were evacuated," Jess said. "They must be staying with friends or relatives. I guess they neglected to call the nursing home."

"I'm glad they're safe. I'll pass the word," Connie said.

"Sam had to go back to SAPD," I said. "His friend Chuck wants to know how his house fared. I told Sam we'd check it out, maybe get started with the cleanup."

He shook his head. "You won't like what you find."

"I know. By the way, when the flood started and you were parked over at the entrance to Turtle Lane, do you remember telling Gwen Highsmith she couldn't go down to Verna and Max Weller's place?"

"Gwen Highsmith…" He thought for a moment, then shrugged. "I'm afraid not. The water was rising so fast, and I was trying to get people out and keep others from going in. I saw so many people that day…."

"I understand."

"I guess you know Max Weller went missing," he said.

"Yes." Did he know Max was dead? Or was he waiting until Verna was notified before making the matter public?

"Poor Verna is so traumatized that Gwen took her to stay Pecan Paradise, but I don't think anyone has told her that Max is missing," I said.

"We're keeping Max's status and Verna's condition private to protect her," Connie said.

"I understand," he said.

"Thanks, Jess."

"Go on in," he said, "but be careful." We pulled onto Lake Placid Drive.

"How did you learn Max is missing?" Connie asked.

"Sam found out. He doesn't think anyone should tell Verna or Gwen yet. He thinks a doctor should be present when they tell Verna."

"I agree."

The road was a nightmare. A Bobcat had scraped heaps of mud to both sides.

We stopped, and Connie snapped pictures. Behind two-foot piles of mud, people's belongings rose in undulating heaps like an endless sea of dark brown sand dunes. Chairs, sofas, clothing, oriental rugs, appliances, framed photos and children's toys were heaped together in the muck. Valuables, mementos, and trinkets of a lifetime created mound after muddy mound of demolished, oversized pickup sticks.

People with grim faces, wearing boots and gloves, shoveled through rubbish, searching for relics of their former lives.

"What a sad sight," Connie said.

About half way down to Chuck's drive, Salvation Army and Red Cross trucks were parked on the right side of the road. Just beyond them, a mud-free driveway was covered with tables and chairs. A couple whose house didn't flood opened their garage and set furniture up on their driveway as a meeting and resting place for neighborhood refugees. A few people sat at tables, their dirty gloves on the ground, nibbling food. Volunteers passed out hand wipes, peanut butter and cheese crackers, and bottles of water.

We drove on. At the end of the road, we saw higher piles of household debris. The area had been inundated by flood waters from two directions. A cut of water from the lake curled around a house-filled peninsula and ran behind houses on the right. As the lake filled and the sky poured, water from the main lake rose from the left and met water coming from the slough on the right.

"That's what happened at my house upriver," Connie said. "The river close to the front of the property curved around behind my house. Water flowed through my home from both sides."

I dreaded what we'd find at Chuck's house.

In front of Alice's house, a man digging through debris flagged us down. I rolled down the window and was hit by a wave of putrid odors.

"Randy Barr," he said. "I'm a friend of Alice Stapleton's."

We introduced ourselves. "Is she all right?"

He laughed. "She's at her sister's house, high and dry, scouring the Seguin *Gazette* for garage sales. She said to come dig for anything worth saving. She couldn't bear to look."

Poor Alice. Her collections had little value before the flood, but they were her treasures. "I don't blame her for not wanting to see this."

"Y'all going farther down? The mud gets higher down there, what with the slough and all."

"We were asked to go check Chuck Atwell's place."

"At least his land is pretty high. Look what happened to houses on the low side." He pointed to the other side of the lake. Across the lake from Chuck's house, two homes had been swept off their foundations. A few standing pillars were the only indications that houses once stood there. One foundation had supported the Wellers' house. Docks were gone or battered beyond repair. Verna, already in shock, had more tragedy to face.

I turned to Randy Barr. "Where do you think those houses ended up?"

"Probably floated over the dam and broke into pieces, like these piles." He waved at the debris. "No telling what the houses hit and took with them. They found stuff all the way from Starke Park down past Lake Nolte."

We shook our heads. Chuck's boat would probably never be found.

"I heard a man from one of those houses disappeared," he said. "Could have drowned, poor guy. I hope they find him alive."

We nodded.

"A woman in a house over there was rescued, but they say she isn't herself."

Connie and I exchanged glances. Alice apparently didn't know about Max or Verna.

"Well," he said, "good luck at Atwell's house." He turned back to the mud pile.

When we reached Chuck's drive, a Bobcat had cleared it and was working on the next driveway down. I made a mental note to pay the driver for his effort. Without him, nobody could get to their homes.

With Connie snapping pictures, we inched toward the low wrought-iron gate leading to Chuck's patio. Mud rose up the side of the houses. We pulled on boots and gloves, grabbed shovels, and started scraping at sticky mud to dislodge enough to open the gate. Five minutes later, we tugged it open.

The patio, a sea of mud a foot-and-a-half deep, extended down the grassy slope to the lake. Where were fish and snakes from the lake? Were they buried in the mud? Was the putrid odor the rotting corpses of lake creatures? I didn't want to think about other corpses.

We slogged through brown, gooey muck toward the door of the big house. Sam hadn't locked it, but we had to dig mud away from the door to get it open. Another ten minutes passed before I could turn the knob.

We stood at the threshold, transfixed by the power of water. Tables and chairs had floated to the living room sofa and lodged against it or floated on top. Lamps, books and trinkets were strewn everywhere. A sheen of river-bottom mud covered the floor. The stench was overwhelming.

"No insurance agent would believe this without photos," Connie said.

In the kitchen, the refrigerator was overturned, opened somehow by the surge of water, and coated with mud. Cabinets and contents were ruined.

"Look up there," Connie said. A line marked the height of muddy water before it receded. Flood water had risen seven feet up the walls. Connie shot pictures of the room from several angles.

This cleanup would take weeks, maybe months. I remembered reading that the strongest predictors of depression after a flood were prior mental health issues, confidence in one's ability to cope, dealing with insurance companies, and the time it took to repair homes. I hoped Chuck Atwell's mental health was good, but at least this was his vacation home, not his family home, full of memories. Dealing with contractors remotely could take a long time. People all over Central Texas would be desperate for help and competing for contractors.

We walked through the cottage on mud-slick floors. Every piece of ruined furniture would have to be hauled out before one could consider cleaning the house. Sinks and toilets, damaged and nasty with river bottom mud, would have to be removed and replaced.

"I wonder if the guest house is this bad," I said. We made our way carefully across the patio. Oddly, the outside of both cottages looked unscathed, as if they'd had a bath.

I pointed to the exterior walls. "Sam said the houses were built in 1948 and '52, and those D'Hanis tile blocks are partially hollow. Maybe muddy water washed over the outside, pressed through the blocks into the houses and settled. The reduced force on the outside structure may have saved the houses from being shoved off the foundations." And killing anyone in their path.

I looked at the joined wooden display boxes attached to the outside of the guest cottage. Each box held a muddy shell or rock as before, including the clamshell Sam put there. Somehow, raging water had washed past them and left the contents intact. I picked up the clamshell, wiped it on my shirt, and placed it back inside the box. Sam and I were forever connected to these houses.

At the entry to the small house, a dead fish was caught between the screen door and the main door, seven feet up.

"Well, we know how high the water got," Connie said. Were there snakes in the mud? I didn't mention the possibility to Connie.

After she snapped a photo, we dug mud away from the door. It took forever to clear enough mud so we could open it. Inside, rank odor assaulted us. The king-size guest bed had floated almost to the ceiling and back down as the water receded. In the middle of the bed, clean clothes lay in plastic bags. They apparently floated up with the bed, protected by being in the center, and floated back down, untouched by receding water. But multiple dry cleanings might never remove the stench.

A row of books on a high shelf behind the bed looked dry but undoubtedly absorbed the smell. I thought about sea water crashing inside houses near the coast. You would have treacherous wind and salt water damage, but no smelly lake-bottom mud.

We peered into the muddied bathroom and continued to the smaller guest bedroom. The only pieces that might be rehabilitated were wrought iron chairs and wicker furniture. Wicker, made of pond fronds, was used to being wet. Everything made with wood or sheetrock was destroyed.

"We can wait for Chuck to get here, or we can try to help," I said.

"The longer this mud stagnates, the worse it will be," Connie said. "We need men to shovel mud off the patio and get it back into the lake."

"And haul furniture and appliances to the curb."

"I feel like we haven't accomplished a thing," she said, "and I'm exhausted."

"Let's go back to the motel and clean up. I'll give Sam the bad news to tell Chuck."

Connie groaned and rolled her neck and shoulders. "I'm too tired to go back to Pecan Paradise. Tanya will have to update me on the residents."

I ached, too. Digging away wet mud was hard work. "You documented the damage for Chuck's insurance company. There's nothing more we can do for now."

# TWENTY

"Will you take me by an office supply store in Seguin before we go to the motel? I'd really like to have my own computer to do research." Thank goodness Sam loaned me his credit card.

"Sure. There's one on Highway 123, right on the way."

In the parking lot, Connie stayed in the car and leaned her head back, prepared to doze. I hurried into the store and spotted the computers. I stopped at each laptop and was checking features when I noticed a salesman at the end of the aisle.

"Can I help you?" he said with a smile. He came toward me and stopped four feet away. His smile wavered.

"I need a moderately priced laptop," I said. "It doesn't need a ton of storage, but I'd like a pretty fast processor."

"That Samsung, two machines to your left, is probably the best for what you need." I expected him to come show me the features. He didn't budge. I approached the Samsung, read about the features and placed my hands on the keyboard.

He coughed and inched backwards. "That's a good product," he said. His eyes watered. "Would you like me to get one for you?"

"You must have terrible allergies," I said.

"I think it's…" He backed away… "Have you been to the flooded areas?"

That's when it hit me. The odor of putrid mud had permeated my clothing. I smelled like rotting fish.

"I'm so sorry. We've been cleaning a lake house. I'll take that computer. When you're ready for me to pay, come to the front entrance. I'll be outside to hand you my credit card."

I think he set a record for locating the boxed computer and making out the ticket. When I handed my card through the door, he looked stricken.

"It's my boyfriend's card. He authorized me to use it."

He hurried away to ring up the purchase. He returned, holding his breath, and handed me the box.

Connie had lowered the windows. We let air gust through the car on our way to the motel and trudged to our rooms.

I washed my hair, body, and clothes, rinsed with pool water, softened my skin with lotion, and dialed Sam.

"It's a mess here," he said. "Lots of people with flooded homes lost their belongings."

"Chuck's house is ruined, Sam. Sheetrock, appliances, bedding, kitchen cabinets, and contents have to be thrown out before he can even think about cleaning the interior. And he'll have to get the mud off the patio before he can do anything inside. Connie took photos of everything."

"I'll let him know. When he called earlier, I didn't know what to tell him, except that it will be bad."

"Even if he has flood insurance, it won't begin to cover the damage."

"I hate that this happened on my watch. What about the neighbors?"

"A man on the road said Alice Stapleton was high, dry, and safe at her sister's house, plotting her next shopping trip. She apparently doesn't know about Verna and Max. When Connie and I go back to the lake tomorrow, we'll visit Garner Ross. Verna Weller looks catatonic and terrified. Gwen comes to see her, but Verna's not talking. Nobody talks about Max, and Verna doesn't ask. Did you get a report from the Medical Examiner?"

"Yes. Because of his wife's fragile condition, they started on Max this afternoon. A preliminary autopsy found alcohol and barbiturates in his system, and he had a blow to the head. It wouldn't have taken much of a hit, maybe debris in the lake, to knock him unconscious. There was water in his lungs, so the ME listed the manner of death as undetermined, and the cause as drowning. I'll find his lawyer and see if he found any other relatives. How are you holding up at Econo-Taj?"

"I'm all right. There's so much to do at the nursing home that we're not here much. I think I'm pickled with chlorine, though. What about Grace?"

"Nothing new, I'm afraid. We can't find any trace of her or Boffo. We found her step-grandson's name… they're looking for his address and telephone number. The more time passes, the worse it looks, Aggie."

"I know. I can't stop hoping."

"No. Don't stop hoping."

"Remember the clam shell, Sam? The one you put in the shadow box on the outside wall? The wall of water just passed it by. I feel like we're tied to that lake house."

"After all we went through, I guess we are."

\* \* \* \* \*

Wednesday morning, Connie and I left early and stopped for an Egg McMuffin on the way to Pecan Paradise. We stopped at the hardware store to purchase seventy-five feet of hose and a sprayer nozzle. Fortunately, most of the lake houses still had electricity, and electric pumps in the lake provided lawn water. We could squirt the lake house furniture to see what was salvageable. Hopefully, we could blast the sheen of mud off paneled walls in the living room and D'Hanis tile walls in the interior.

When Connie started her rounds, I decided to see Verna. I was almost to her room when Art Lively came toward me down the hall.

"Hello, Art. How is Verna?"

He shook his head. "Sad. So very sad." He plodded away, looking very different from the exuberant host of the home-owners' meeting.

Gwen came out of Verna's room and closed the door. "She's sleeping peacefully," she said. "Seeing Art was probably good for her, even though she didn't respond. He did all the talking. She's probably exhausted. You're not planning to visit today, are you?"

"I guess not, if she's asleep."

Gwen paused as if considering whether to reveal something. "After Art's wife left him years ago, he and Verna were pretty close," she said. "Then Max showed up and broke them up."

All the men attracted to Verna lived on the lake. She couldn't seem to escape it. Had she repressed her fear of living lakeside and acted content knowing Gwen wished she was back in Seguin?

"I remember," I said, "at the homeowners' meeting, how Garner pressed Max to re-build their house so Verna wouldn't be afraid to live there."

"Garner Sledge will say anything to talk people into selling or re-doing their homes. But Verna didn't have to stay there. She could leave or tell Max to leave. It was *her* house."

"I never thought of it that way."

"I've got errands to run before I get back to the school. See you later, Aggie."

I went to the kitchen and found Connie. Residents were eating lunch in the dining room. Connie and I were hungry for cheese sandwiches and ate at the kitchen table.

"After a couple more days of cleaning out mud, we'll be ready for a night out," I said. "Let's find the nicest place to eat and go there for dinner tomorrow night. My treat."

"I can't turn that down. How about The Huisache Grill in New Braunfels? It's only been open a few years, but they say it's great."

We were surprised to see Gwen standing in the doorway. With a nod, she grabbed a banana off the counter. "Sustenance for running errands and facing kids." We smiled as she hustled away.

"The Huisache Grill. Now I have something to look forward to," I said. "Ready to face the mud?"

# TWENTY-ONE

Officer Perez's patrol car was gone from the subdivision entrance. A sign was posted: ENTRANCE FOR LAKE PLACID RESIDENTS ONLY. NO TRESSPASSING. I couldn't imagine anyone wanting to go in. There was nothing left, even for looters.

We saw signs of progress along the road, driveways cleared of mud and people in boots squirting off houses. Residents still carried ruined treasures to the street, and the piles had grown higher. People hauled plastic buckets loaded with bleach, liquid cleaner, brushes, brooms, and thick plastic bags. Like a village of fishermen, clammers, or lobstermen, they plodded through the neighborhood, cleaning their own houses or helping others. As soon as the county sent trucks to pick up the mounds of destroyed possessions, it would feel like a major step forward.

As we neared our driveway, we stopped beside two pickups. One truck bed was filled with wheelbarrows and the other with college kids. "Need some help?" they called. "We can scoop your mud into the lake."

"That would be great. Where are you from?"

"Texas Lutheran College in Seguin. The school gave us a week off to help flood victims."

Connie snapped pictures. They followed us and got to work scooping mud into wheelbarrows and pushing them toward the lake. I'd be a supporter of TLU forever.

Connie and I connected the hose and squirted off wrought iron and wicker furniture. I found my purse, but it and the contents were ruined, except for my driver's license and a credit card. I'd already bought a new wallet and used Sam's credit card to get cash at an ATM. The kids said to put damaged goods in the back of their pickup, and the boys hauled heavy pieces to the street.

Two hours later, the patio was passable and nearly mud-free. Both houses were empty except for large appliances. While the kids reloaded wheelbarrows into their truck, Connie and I expressed thanks, opened our wallets and told them they definitely earned hamburgers. After they ate, they said they'd come back to help other neighbors.

We tried squirting interior tile walls, but our sprayer didn't have enough power to blast off sticky residue. We'd have to rent a power washer.

I walked underneath the patio cover and looked across the lake. It looked like a war zone. Mud still covered the road behind what remained of the homes, so people couldn't enter the subdivision to clean up. How could we ever find out what happened to Max or Chuck's boat? Raging water had swept clues over the dam.

"Let's go see how Garner Sledge is doing," Connie said. To avoid bogging down in the muddy lawn between houses, we walked to the road. We saw the man with the Bobcat and went to offer cash and thanks, then walked up Garner's driveway. He sloshed around his cars, cursing.

"Gosh dang water left me enough mud to plant a rice field."

"Students from TLU are coming back in an hour or so to scrape it up and wheel it back to the lake," I said pleasantly.

"I wondered why they took off. Can't count on kids to work anymore."

"Pushing wheelbarrows loaded with mud is hard work, and they went to grab lunch," Connie said. "Besides, they're doing it for nothing. The school gave them a week off to help."

"They probably weren't studying anyway."

The TLU kids might not last long at Grumpy's place. "Did you get water upstairs in your house?"

"About a foot. With mud, of course."

"We had it too. Along with seven feet of water." I couldn't keep the edge out of my voice. "Have you heard anything about other neighbors? If they survived the flood or lost homes?"

"How do I know what happened to anybody? I've got a colossal mess here." He shoved muddy water away from his cars with a push broom.

"The students should be back soon," Connie said. "Wouldn't hurt to tip them when they finish." We walked back down his drive. "At least cleaning up his mess will keep him from trying to buy property cheap for a while," Connie muttered.

"Let's drive down to the Salvation Army and Red Cross trucks," I said, "and hang out with charitable people."

By four thirty in the afternoon, everyone on Lake Placid was tired and hungry. Refugees cleaning uninhabitable homes had gathered at tables set up in the Touheys' driveway. We pulled up behind the trucks and walked over. Volunteers placed hand sanitizer, bottles of water, and peanut butter and cheese crackers on the tables. Somebody put a money pot in the center of a table and we chipped in.

Lake dwellers cleaned their hands and arms as best they could and lined up with paper plates where the owners filled them with home-made lasagna. We sat at a table for eight, introduced ourselves, and tore into the best lasagna we'd ever eaten.

A cool, dry breeze wafted through the tables, as if to uplift soggy spirits. After a few minutes, people began telling their stories in low tones. As visitors, we stayed silent and listened.

"One man, four or five houses down river from me, rented a small house and had a camper in the drive. When water flooded his home, he climbed up on the roof of the camper. Somebody rescued him from there. He'd been a POW in Vietnam, but he said watching that water rise up to him was more frightening that anything he saw in 'Nam. After the flood, he left the area. Said he was never coming back."

"Y'all know Gunther and Ida Schmidt?" A few of us nodded. "Somebody plucked them off their roof. They're with their children in New Braunfels and are looking for a house."

That made me smile. Another man starting speaking.

"Our house is ruined. We had the house and contents insured for flood damage, but the agent says FEMA will probably give us about a third of the amount we insured for. FEMA says we have to build a house up on stilts high enough that a five-hundred-year flood can go under it."

"What's a five-hundred-year flood?"

"In any given year, there's a one-in-five-hundred chance that another flood like this will occur."

"Is it true FEMA gives money to people who live in flood plains to elevate their houses?"

"Yeah. But what if their houses are forty years old, like ours? Does it make sense to spend taxpayer money to elevate a forty-year-old house? If FEMA let you put that money toward building a new elevated house, it might make sense."

"Government programs don't always make sense. FEMA will probably run out of money anyway."

It sounded like Sam's friend, Chuck Atwell, didn't have many options. None of them good.

"Well, it's happened before. I heard about a couple who lost everything in the '87 flood. They had enough savings to rent a hotel room in Seguin until they could pull themselves together and decide what to do next. The wife wanted to talk about what happened—let it out. But her husband refused to discuss it. They had things to do, he said. Best thing was to get on with their lives and not dwell on it. She'd go into the shower at night and talk to herself about the flood. I heard she's in some kind of facility now and can't speak."

It was 5:30 when we left Lake Placid for the motel. "Do you think they were talking about Verna?" I asked.

"Could be anybody. It might have been a guest who stayed in a nursing home for a while and left. Do you think we can get clean in an hour?"

I glanced down at my muddy jeans and shirt. "I might get the top two layers of mud off."

Connie laughed. "I'll knock on your door about 6:30."

# TWENTY-TWO

I bathed and dressed fast as I could so I'd have time to call Sam. Even my new clothes smelled like chlorine. I used my hair dryer to blow away the odor, then applied powder and mascara. I dialed Sam's number.

"Any news about Grace?" I asked.

"I'm afraid not. They tried to contact her step-grandson and his family, but neighbors say they're traipsing around Australia. Their contact information for him isn't good for two weeks."

I swallowed the lump in my throat. It was a while before I could answer. "I can't bear to think about losing her, Sam."

"I know. The whole department is on notice to look for her."

I sniffled and dabbed at the tears welling in the corners of my eyes with a tissue, then tilted my new makeup mirror to the magnification side to see if tears had smudged my mascara.

"Since Art Lively hosts the poker game, I decided to give him a call," Sam said. "I thought he might know Max's lawyer and anybody who'd showed interest in Chuck's boat. He said Max lost so much money to Garner Sledge playing poker that Sledge kept records of how much he owed. He demanded that Max put in his will that his estate pay his debt to Sledge first."

"Why would Max agree to that?"

"All Max liked to do was fish and play poker. He owed all the guys money. They told him they'd kick him out of the game if he didn't do what Sledge said. It's a small community, and

Max would be ostracized. Art went with Max to his lawyer to witness the agreement. The lawyer had to know it wouldn't withstand legal scrutiny, but I guess since they both insisted, he added it in."

My thoughts whirled. "So Garner had a financial reason to kill Max?"

"More like a personal vendetta. But there's more. When Rick Crane, the game warden, called me about Max's death, he relayed an interesting story."

"About Garner?"

"Yeah. It seems that Crane's fellow Game Warden, Joe Ramirez, served in Vietnam in the same Marine unit as Garner Sledge. Sledge went AWOL. Said he just didn't want to fight in that war."

"He *what*? After all that stuff about being proud to serve?"

"You got it. None of those boys wanted to be fighting a war. But they went and did the best they could. Anyway, when Sledge went missing, the whole unit risked their lives searching for him. They brought him back all skinny and dehydrated."

I stifled a laugh. "Hard to imagine Garner Sledge skinny."

"Yeah." Sam chuckled. "Well, when they were out searching for Sledge, Ramirez's best buddy was killed by an IED. The Marines downplayed the details, but everybody in the unit knew what happened. Word got out to other units in 'Nam. Max and Joe Ramirez were drinking beer one night, and Ramirez told Max that Garner Sledge deserted."

"So Garner had another reason to want Max dead."

"Yep. If Max told everybody about him, Sledge would lose his upstanding place in the community and probably his real estate business."

I snorted. "And he'd have to remove the picture of himself in Marine uniform from his entry hall."

"That, too."

I heard a knock on the door. "Connie's here, Sam. We going to treat ourselves to dinner in New Braunfels. You've given me a lot to chew on. I'll call you in the morning. Love you."

I opened the door smiling and gave a tentative sniff. "Why don't you smell like chlorine?" I asked.

Connie grinned. "The water is back on at the retirement home. We have a washer and dryer. Do you mind stopping by there a few minutes?"

I shook my head.

She continued. "I need to give last-minute instructions to Tanya. Bring your clothes. She can add them to other loads, and you can pick them up tomorrow."

"You're an angel!" I gathered my clothes and carried them to the car.

The roads were busy. Everyone must be out looking for supplies and checking storm damage. When we arrived at the home, I handed my clothes to Tanya, along with my heartfelt thanks.

While Connie talked with Tanya, I decided to visit Verna. Maybe hearing good news from the lake would cheer her. I peeked in

"Hi, Verna. How are you doing? I've been down to the lake and thought you might like an update."

She looked at me, or through me. I wasn't sure which.

I told her about the Red Cross and Salvation Army trucks and the Touheys setting up a place to rest and eat in their driveway, about Guenther and Ida being saved from their roof and safe with their children in New Braunfels, and how TLU college students pitched in to clean up. A corner of her mouth curled up in a semi-smile.

I was so astonished, I smiled back. She turned abruptly toward the window.

"Okay. I'll see you later, Verna. Get well."

When I opened the door to the hall, Gwen was there.

"Hello, Aggie. I didn't expect to see you this late."

"We just stopped in on our way to dinner. I was telling Verna about the good things happening at Lake Placid. I'm not sure… it was only a split second… but I think she almost smiled."

"Ah, yes. She does that. The next minute, she starts screaming frantically about something. She's inconsolable." She sighed. "I don't even know what upsets her."

"I'm so sorry. I better let you check on her. Connie is probably waiting for me in the lobby." I smiled. "I'm starving. I think I ingested a tape worm cleaning out mud."

# TWENTY-THREE

In twenty minutes, Connie and I were in New Braunfels at The Huisache Grill, seated at a table and clinking glasses of chardonnay.

"Did I tell you I saw Art Lively after he visited Verna?" I said. "He looked shocked at her condition. Gwen said he dated Verna until Max entered the picture."

"Art knows everybody on the lake. He sells them insurance," Connie said. She took a sip of wine. "He's even the agent for FEMA's flood insurance. Because Max was out alone on the lake all the time, Art sold him a life insurance policy."

I had to concentrate to keep the shock off my face. My feet itched. Connie didn't know Max was dead, let alone possibly murdered. Did Art want Max dead so he could re-establish his relationship with Verna and help her spend the insurance?

I told myself not to gulp the next glass of wine. We had a delicious dinner, and let time slip away. We talked about everybody on the lake and about Connie's residents.

"They adore you, you know," she said. "They love it when you show up at the lounge to play games."

"I enjoy them. They're so welcoming and honest. I think they're beyond the point of trying to impress."

She grinned. "They say pretty much what's on their mind. You should come work for me. Seriously."

I frowned. "I couldn't do that. I have a house and a job, and Sam's there. But I'm flattered."

"Didn't you say your house will take months to repair?" she said. "And can't you write from anywhere? I imagine you and Sam can cover thirty-five miles from here to San Antonio pretty fast."

"Well, yes, but…"

"Think about it. We need somebody the residents enjoy, who's not busy operating the facility."

"Okay. I will." That would be a lot of change in a short time. But I did love the lake… and these people.

My mind flipped to Verna and Max's various relationships. They were all intertwined, the lake dwellers, with shared tragedies and entangled jealousies. The list of people who might want Max Weller dead was growing. He had dumped Alice, Verna didn't like living on the lake, and Gwen wished Alice still lived in Seguin. Art sold him life insurance, he owned Garner and the other players money, and Max knew about Garner's desertion. For a guy who just wanted to fish, Max had alienated a lot of people.

I felt fatigue setting in. "I think I'll use the ladies' room before we start back. I'll probably fall into bed when we get home."

By the time we left The Huisache Gill, it was dark. We made it to Econo-Taj and trudged to our rooms. My habitat still smelled like chlorine, but I didn't really care. I was getting used to it. I didn't bother about my makeup, stripped off my clothes, and slipped under the sheets.

* * * * *

Sam and I were clasped in each other's arms inside Chuck's lake house. The house had slid down the slope into the lake and floated inexorably toward the dam. I was starting to panic when I heard Grace's voice.

"You're not in the lake," she said in her calm voice. "You're having lunch at the table down on the dock. The water is lapping gently underneath. The sky is full of fluffy blue clouds and the sun is just strong enough to warm you from the breeze."

I imagined the scene, feeling soothed.

"Want to hear what I'm doing?" she said.

"Sure."

"I've been spending a lot of time with my beloved Ray, but he thought we should cool it for a while, so I could deal with issues from my past."

"Issues?"

"Yes, you know. My first two husbands. Why Charlie did what he did. If he felt remorseful. If they have him doing penance. What I felt about the person who did him in. Things like that."

"You told me about Charlie, but I remember you had unanswered questions. So. Where you are now, do people do penance for what they did?"

"The Boss decides, of course. You can get here, but escaping the choices you made? That's something else. We all have to deal with that. They let you settle in first. Learn why other people did what they did. They hope it helps you before you start on yourself."

"You have to deal with everything you did?"

"Of course. Nobody's perfect. Except for Him. He had me start with Charlie, since his motivations are so hard to understand. Then there's George. I didn't understand him either. That's why I have to work on it now, like what actually happened when *he* died… where the pills came from, things like that. The biggie is why I married them in the first place."

"That's a good question," I said.

Grace laughed. "The interesting thing is that everybody here tells you the unvarnished truth. They can't help it. It takes a while getting used to. I'll keep you posted on my progress. Right now, you need to get up. Open the patio door."

I waited for more, but Grace's voice faded. I blinked my eyes open to blackness. Boy, did I have to go to the bathroom. I had to shake myself awake enough to get out of bed. The door to the bathroom was closed, and the toilet seat was down. I lifted the seat and sat. Fumes made me instantly dizzy and nauseous.

As soon as I could, I staggered out of the bathroom, lurched across the bedroom, and lunged for the patio door. Sliding it open, I lurched to the outside rail and leaned over. My head began to clear. What was I doing? I might tumble over the rail. I stumbled backward to the wall, almost tripping over the drowned potted plant placed there before the storm to add a tropical touch. I closed the patio door. Clutching at the bricks, I slid to the floor and let the night air blow across my face.

I couldn't go back into that room. If I climbed over the rail and fell, I'd land on concrete. I needed help. Connie was in the next room. I scooted toward it. Five feet separated my patio rail from hers, too far for me to reach it. I scooted toward the potted plant. The container was plastic. If I could extract the soggy plant, maybe I could throw the pot over and hit Connie's patio door.

Fighting to stay conscious, I pushed the pot onto its side and started digging. I clawed out enough sodden dirt to take out the plant.

With my feet, I pushed the empty pot to the rail. Could I stand up, pick up the pot and heave it toward her window before I passed out?

I stood and steadied myself against the rail, praying for strength. I would need both hands to hurl the pot. When I bent to pick up the pot, I grew dizzy. I grabbed the rail, tugged the pot up with my other hand and set it on the rail against my chest. Could I let go of the rail long enough to throw it?

Moving the pot with me, I inched toward the brick wall. When my back touched the wall, I leaned against it. Grabbing the lip of the pot with both hands, I flung it at Connie's patio door. I heard it hit the glass before I slid down the wall and blacked out.

# TWENTY-FOUR

I woke up on the lawn in front of Econo-Taj on a stretcher. I peered down at the oxygen mask over my nose and mouth.

"What happened?" I mumbled. "Why is this thing on my face?"

Connie motioned to an EMS guy. "She can talk now. Can we take this off?"

He removed the plastic cone from my face and grabbed my wrist to take my pulse. "What's her name?"

"Aggie. Aggie Mundeen."

"Miss Mundeen, I want you to answer some questions for me." He asked me my name (which he knew), my address (which was problematic since I'd been displaced), where I was (which was pretty obvious) and how I felt. Much better than I did in the bathroom.

"Can you tell me what happened?"

"I was in my hotel room, went to the bathroom and was overcome by fumes that made me nauseous and light headed. I staggered to the patio balcony for air and threw a plastic pot at Connie's patio door so she would wake up and help me. I must have blacked out. I woke up on the lawn. Can I sit up?"

"Yes. Slowly. Sit here a while. We'll come back and check on you." Dr. Billups, from the ER, came over. He must be moonlighting for EMS. I'd recognize his twelve-year-old face anywhere. He asked me the same questions, put his stethoscope on my chest and an oxygen-saturation gadget on my finger and took my pulse.

"You seem fine. You've spent a lot of time in a prone position lately."

"I know. I don't usually. Just a series of unusual events."

He grinned. "We've got to stop meeting like this."

"Right." I grinned. "Thanks, Dr. Billups." He whirled and walked toward an EMS person.

I turned to Connie. "Did you have fumes in your room?"

"No. They evacuated the hotel, but according to EMS, the problem was apparently localized to your bathroom."

"The chlorine smell was really strong."

"Yes, but it was mixed with something. EMS called HAZMAT from San Antonio. They're analyzing the substance. EMS gave me your phone, so I called Sam. He's on the way."

"Poor guy. Nothing like working a long day, then getting a call in the middle of the night."

"It might be less startling than having a pot crash against your patio door when you were in a dead sleep." She grinned. "I told Sam I thought you were okay. He insisted on coming."

I smiled. We watched HAZMAT talk to EMS.

"I know some of the EMS guys who've made trips to Pecan Paradise. Maybe they'll tell me what they found." She got up and walked toward a man, they talked a few minutes, and she threaded her way back. "HAZMAT said it was a mixture of chlorine and ammonia. They're found in common cleaning products, but the combination can be lethal. Police are checking out hotel employees and guests. From what they know now, the mixture was only in your toilet, no others."

"I remember now. The door to the bathroom was closed and the toilet seat was down. I guess the mixture was contained until I opened everything up."

"Somebody poured chlorine and ammonia in your toilet and lowered the seat and closed the bathroom door to confine the fumes. You were lucky to get out of there."

Why would anyone want me dead? I spotted Sam zigzagging around people sitting on the lawn as fast as he could, carrying a plastic bag. When he found me, I smiled.

He squatted down and stared at me intently, hair flopping on his forehead. "Are you okay?"

I nodded. I loved that floppy hair.

"Are you sure? Did EMS check you out? Did a doctor look at you?"

"Yes, yes, and yes. What's in the bag?"

"Clean clothes with soap, shampoo, a toothbrush, toothpaste, and an extra pair of my pajamas. And I got us a room at a new motel on I-10. It even has hot running water."

"Awesome."

People on the lawn began to stand up and leave. EMS and HAZMAT were packing up, and two Seguin police officers arrived. I recognized Jess Perez, and Sam walked over to him.

"Since the police ransacked my room, and you two are okay," Connie said, "I think I'll go to Pecan Paradise and sleep there. Why don't you call me tomorrow?"

I hugged her. "Thank you, Connie. I could never have done without you these past days... or last night."

"You helped me, too," she said, "and my residents. Maybe you should organizae a bean bag toss tournament for them." She smiled and left.

When Sam finished talking with Jess Perez, he took my arm, and we walked to his car. I sank into the passenger seat, grateful to be alive. I could have died.

Sam started the car. "You want to tell me what you did today before this happened?"

"We went by Pecan Paradise and the lake house and came here to clean up for dinner. Connie and I went to eat at The Huisache Grill in New Braunfels. Do you remember I told you that Art dated Verna before Max entered the picture? Connie said that Art knows everybody on the lake because he sells them insurance, even FEMA flood insurance. And because Max was out on the lake all the time, Art also sold him life insurance."

"Hmm. Art failed to mention that. But he gave me the name of Max's lawyer who told me that Verna's first husband,

Bob, left her the lake house. When Max wanted to marry her and move in, she was afraid the house would become community property. So she had her lawyer draw up a document that in the event Max died, was incapacitated, or abandoned her, Verna would own the house. She had Gwen there for support and to witness Max's signature."

"I'm surprised, because Verna didn't like to live on the lake."

Sam nodded. "True. But Max wasn't very sympathetic with Verna's fear of living there."

"That reminds me of a story Connie and I heard after cleaning at the lake. A couple escaped the '87 flood from Pecan Cove subdivision, but their house was destroyed. The husband was so upset, he forbade his wife to discuss their experience. Maybe that's why Verna has PTSD. She was commanded not to speak about it and now can't bear to relive the experience."

"Max couldn't have forbade her from discussing the flood," Sam said. "He was gone."

"It could have been Bob," I said, "her first husband. And Verna's fear mushroomed."

Sam thought for a long time before he spoke. "After we clean up and get a few hours sleep, we need to make an early stop at Pecan Paradise."

# TWENTY-FIVE

We woke at seven, found the nearest Denny's for a hearty breakfast and then headed for Pecan Paradise.

"I didn't want to ruin your breakfast after your first night with hot running water," Sam said, glancing at me, "but I got Max's autopsy report. He hit his head but that's not what killed him. He had a lethal amount of Cardizem in his body"

I stared at him. "Wow. What's that for?"

"To lower blood pressure or reduce chest pain. It relaxes blood vessels in the heart and body and lowers the heart rate."

I thought for a moment. "Did Max have high blood pressure or cardiac issues?"

"I don't know. He was overweight, took barbiturates, and drank alcohol. Taking Cardizem could give him a slow or irregular heart beat and make him feel faint or dizzy—not good if he fell in a raging river."

"No. He'd never have a chance."

"There's more. Game wardens found Chuck's boat down below the dam past Lake Nolte. It was smashed up, but the tag numbers on the side looked new. They took them for DNA analysis and compared them to Max's DNA. It was a match."

"So Max stole Chuck's boat before the flood?"

He nodded. "He could have taken it anytime the week before."

"Why?"

He shrugged. "He loved boats and fishing gear. Probably thought Chuck's boat was better than his. Maybe he planned to sell it to pay his gambling debts."

We arrived at Pecan Paradise. "By the way," he said, "I met Dr. Billups last night on the lawn and asked him to stop by Verna's room. I hope we find Gwen there. I want to watch both women's reactions when we tell them about Max. I'm beginning to wonder if one of them had something to do with his death."

I was shocked. "But Verna was his wife. If she didn't love him, she could have told him to leave. Gwen told me the house belonged to Verna. And why would Gwen kill her sister's husband? She's always taking care of Verna. The last time I saw Gwen, she looked exhausted. I know she's worried about Verna and is probably not eating well. Connie says she's diabetic."

"Maybe I'm wrong," Sam said.

As we entered the lobby of Pecan Paradise, my phone rang. Before I could answer, Tanya ran up to us, pale and shaking. "I just called you. Connie was taking inventory and is frantic. Cleaning supplies are missing, and somebody took meds from the medication locker!"

Sam wasn't usually wrong. What he said about Verna and Gwen frightened me. I ran to Verna's room, and Sam overtook me. We burst through the door and froze. Gwen towered over Verna, holding a syringe.

I shouted at Verna. "Roll away from the needle!"

Sam lunged at Gwen, knocked the syringe out of her hand and put her in a choke hold.

"I'm trying to save her," Gwen gurgled. "Cure her of PTSD. Let me go!"

Verna rolled out of bed and backed up against the wall, crying and staring at Gwen.

"You're all right, aren't you, Verna?" I said.

She nodded.

Sam glared at Gwen. "Looks like you found an instant cure for PTSD."

Connie charged into the room followed by Dr. Billups and Jess Perez with a set of handcuffs. He went straight to Gwen and cuffed her.

I looked at Sam. "How did…?"

"I called Jess before breakfast."

Gwen stared at Sam and paled. "You're a cop?"

He nodded.

Gwen's eye's narrowed. She glared at me with pure hatred. "I thought you asked too many questions." Her mouth curled with disgust. "So your boyfriend is a cop."

"Get dressed, Miss Verna," Jess said. "We'll need to talk with you later."

"We'll help her," Connie and I said.

Keeping an eye on Gwen, Sam picked up the syringe.

I turned to Connie. "Are you missing insulin from medical supply?"

She nodded. "And Cardizem."

"Will insulin kill someone who isn't diabetic?" I asked Dr. Billups.

"No doubt," he said.

Connie looked stricken.

While Sam and Officer Perez took Gwen to the patrol car, we helped Verna dress. Dr. Billups checked her out and left. When Sam returned, Verna sat on her bed, crying. Connie and I stood on either side.

"She can't believe what Gwen did," I told Sam, "but she's perfectly lucid."

He looked at her. "Tell us what happened, Verna."

She sniffed. "I'd been telling Gwen how Max slept less and less. He'd wake up at night, screaming about Vietnam. He was keeping me awake all night, and he never wanted to do anything in the daytime but fish." She turned to me. "I told you his meds helped him sleep, but they really didn't."

She looked at Sam. "He said he'd never leave the lake house. Gwen tried to hide her feelings, but she resented him for it. Friday night, she said she'd bring something to help him sleep. He was drinking when she came, so she put it in his beer."

"Did that worry you?" Sam said.

"Not really. I thought Gwen was being helpful. But later, they started arguing about our living at the lake. I begged them to stop shouting. It was pitch dark and thundering, and they got louder and louder. It must have been after midnight when Max grabbed a raincoat and stormed out on the dock. Gwen grabbed my raincoat and followed. They kept on shouting."

She blinked away tears. "I tried to see them in the dark through the window. When lightning flashed on the dock, they were gone."

"Did you go outside to look for them?" I asked.

"I started to, but Gwen came into the kitchen and said Max fell into the river—that it was an accident. She called 9-1-1 and we waited. Neither of us are good swimmers, the lake was churning, and it looked like a storm was brewing. We didn't know what else to do. We waited and waited. I don't know why nobody came. By the wee hours Saturday morning, we were losing hope. Finally, Gwen said, 'He's gone. We need to accept it. Since it was an accident, nobody needs to know he and I were out there together. We'll just say he went out on the dock and never came back.'"

Sam and I looked at each other. Why did Verna believe Gwen?

"Gwen said she was going home," Verna said. "She urged me to take one of Max's barbiturates so I could sleep and said neither of us should talk about what happened."

Maybe Verna wanted Max gone.

"The deluge really hadn't started yet," Verna said. "Gwen said Max was a strong swimmer and would be okay. The next morning when it started to rain, I was groggy. The river began to flood, water flowed into the house, and somebody got me out. The next thing I knew I was here at Pecan Paradise."

"Was Gwen here when you woke up?" I asked.

"Yes. She must have left after I went to bed. After I was rescued, somebody who knew we were sisters called her."

"When you work up at the hospital, she described PTSD symptoms and told you to act like you had them," Sam said.

"Gwen thought it was better. She knew I was traumatized from the flood. That way, I wouldn't have to deal with a bunch of questions.

"Did you wonder why you were at Pecan Paradise?" I asked Verna.

"Verna said our doctor okayed it with Connie until I recovered from the flood."

Connie nodded. "She gave me their doctor's written orders."

Verna sobbed into her hands. "That's when I realized Max was still missing. I don't know what I'm going to do."

"You can stay here as long as you like," Connie said. "I'll be right here."

Connie had a good heart, but Verna probably had insurance to pay for it.

"Officer Perez will want you to give a statement at headquarters," Sam said. "I'll call your attorney and have him meet you there. I suggest you don't say anything on the way to Police Headquarters. The first person you talk to should be your attorney."

# TWENTY-SIX

Sam and I drove down I-10 to our motel in silence. There was a lot to process. When we reached the parking lot, I turned to him. "I need fresh air. Since it's not raining, let's sit by the pool."

We walked through the lobby to the pool, and Sam found us spring chairs.

"I think I know why Gwen wanted to kill Verna," I said. "For all her apparent dislike of the lake house, she wanted it."

Sam nodded.

"Now I realize she hated Max," I said, "hated the way he controlled Verna."

"She probably controlled Verna herself until Max showed up and took over," he said.

I remembered being eager to monopolize Sam for the weekend. Maybe for longer than that. Was I turning into a Gwen? I shuddered.

"So even though Max fell into the water," I said, "Gwen killed him."

"Looks that way. At the least, the drug she gave him made him fall into the water and unable to help himself."

"As a nurse, she would know that would happen," I said. "And the flood washed away traces of the drug and beer bottles."

"Gwen probably faked calling 9-1-1," Sam said. "We can check their records."

"Gwen conjured up more schemes," I said. "She must have talked the visiting nurse at Pecan Paradise into letting her unlock the medical supply cabinet to 'get something' for Verna."

"And she took the syringe of insulin," he said. "An autopsy doesn't show insulin, since it's in the body anyway. She probably got the Cardizem another time, and they just discovered it was missing. Both drugs are common in nursing homes."

"I bet the cleaning supplies Connie discovered missing are Clorox and ammonia," I said, "and that Gwen has empty bottles at her house wiht her prints on them."

"I wouldn't be surprised," he said." Jess can check with the doctor who Gwen said ordered Verna's admission to Pecan Paradise. Gwen probably gave forged orders to Connie."

I nodded. "When Gwen overheard Connie and me talk about going to dinner, she must have managed to pick the lock to my hotel room and put the stuff in the toilet. But why did she want to kill me?"

He shrugged. "You kept visiting Verna and you asked a lot of questions. Gwen probably feared you were getting too close to her sister."

"Since Verna never had PTSD and Gwen told her to fake the symptoms," I said, "maybe she and Gwen plotted together to kill Max."

"It's possible, but I'm inclined to believe Verna's story. I suspect she was weakening in her ruse to fake PTSD. Gwen feared she was about to tell what really happened and decided she had to kill her. For all Gwen knew, Verna could say she saw Gwen push Max into the lake."

"If Gwen is convicted of trying to kill Verna, what will happen to her?"

"First-degree attempted murder usually means a life sentence. Offenders typically spend at least ten years in prison. But there's the possibility of parole."

"Verna will have to dispose of what's left of her lake property."

"Ironically, I wouldn't be surprised if she ends up living in Gwen's house in Seguin."

"Speaking of where to live, Sam, there's something I need to tell you."

He raised his eyebrows until the shock of hair covered them. It was hard for me to go on.

"I've decided to stay here and help Connie with the nursing home."

He leaned forward, his eyes wide open. "I thought you wanted us to be together."

"I do. But my Burr Road home isn't habitable. And your apartment is… it's for a man."

I'd made my decision, but it was hard to express. "My happiness shouldn't depend on your letting me help with investigations. People here need me, Sam. Connie needs help. Residents at Pecan Paradise need to interact with people who like them. I saw family members act like visiting was a chore. I have an important job to do here."

"I need you, too."

"Sometimes. But you do your job quite well without me. And I'm only thirty minutes away."

"But…"

"Connie will rent me a room and bath in the nursing home as long as I need it. She'll pay me as a member of the staff." I paused to look at him. He still didn't understand. "Connie gets sustenance from helping people, Sam. I want to *be* like that."

"I didn't know you felt that way."

"I didn't know it either. I guess tragedy makes you re-evaluate everything, especially when you survive and others don't. I always thought of myself as a survivor. But I learned part of truly being a survivor is helping other people learn to survive. And I can help refurbish the lake house."

"You don't need to do that. Chuck can hire contractors."

"I can work with them. Make sure things go well. I feel like it's partly our place, Sam. We survived the flood there. I learned to be a survivor there. I'll love helping bring the lake house back to life."

He sighed. "I'll ask Chuck if he'd like you to oversee the project. I think he'll be grateful and glad to pay for repairs." He studied the concrete around the pool. He accepted my decision, but I still wasn't sure he understood.

"I love you for who you are, Sam. I don't want to love you because you raise my self-esteem by letting me help you investigate. I need to be my own person. I see a way to do that."

"Aggie," he said, "at this moment, I love you more than I've ever loved you." He walked over, raised me from my chair and kissed me. He hugged me for such a long time that he started thinking and drew back. "What about your San Antonio bungalow?"

"I'll find contractors to start repairs. For Grace's house too, if she… if she…." My voice cracked.

"Can I see you on weekends?"

"Of course. I'll never stop loving you, Sam." I grinned. "And you can help me clean out the lake house."

"I'm not sure where we'll stay with everything being repaired."

"There's always Econo-Taj."

He laughed. "That's not going to happen."

His phone rang. "Somebody from SAPD," he said, putting the phone to his ear. "This is Sam."

He listened intently, and his mouth formed a smile. He hung up. I stared at him, waiting.

"That was good news about Grace," he said. "Police found her behind some bushes on Burr Road right after the flood. She's been in a coma at Methodist Hospital, but is waking up. She apparently went after Boffo, fell and blacked out. They found Boffo later. The local vet is boarding him. Doctors think she'll fully recover."

"Take me there. Take me there now!"

# TWENTY-SEVEN

We drove back to San Antonio on I-10, listening to WOAI radio.

*The flood of 1998 was the least-covered major flood in Central Texas. Reporters couldn't get anywhere near the Guadalupe River lakes. All roads were impassible. Extreme rain came from south of Canyon Lake over San Antonio, San Marcos, New Braunfels, Seguin, Gonzales, Wimberley, and Blanco and stalled, flooding rivers and lakes. Twenty-nine inches of rain created 130,000 to 180,000 cubic feet of water per second. This was the highest amount of rain ever to fall over the Guadalupe River Basin in history. The water peaked downstream in Cuero, Victory, and Calhoun with flow rates of 460,000 to 475,000 cubic feet per second.*

At Methodist Hospital, we found Grace's room.

"I think I should wait outside," he said. "Let me know."

I went into the room. Grace's hair was longer. White strands, streaming among the gray, lay on her pillow. She was pale but slept peacefully.

My eyes filled. "Grace, it's Aggie."

Her lids fluttered, and she opened her eyes.

"Grace, you're back. Thank God."

She smiled. "I was never gone. We've been talking. Don't you remember?"

She smiled again, closed her eyes and lapsed into sleep. She couldn't go. Not now. She was my mother, my rock, my wisdom. She'd always been there with her wise counsel. I watched her chest rise and fall in a rhythmical, steady pattern.

I took a deep breath, thankful she could rest. Maybe now, we could both recover.

# ACKNOWLEDGEMENTS

This book is fiction, but the disaster that prompted me to write it was very real: the Central Texas Flood of 1998. My heartfelt thanks go to these people who lived through it and shared memories of that calamitous October weekend. To honor those who suffered loss, friends, neighbors and Texas Lutheran University students who pitched in to clean up damage and mend spirits, and first responders who saved countless lives, my book royalties will go to the Texas Game Warden Association and the 100 Club.

- Doug Parker, Retired Texas Game Warden
- Joe Vega, Retired Texas Game Warden
- Dan and Jennifer Dykstra, father and daughter who survived hours stranded on top of lake debris
- Forrest M. Mims III, scientist, writer and photographer
- Debra Baumler, Former Administrator, Long Term Care, Seguin, Texas nursing home
- Darrell Hunter, formerly with Seguin PD, currently Justice of the Peace
- Darren Dunn, Manager, KWED Radio, Seguin
- Mark Lenz, Service Hydrologist, National Weather Service Austin/San Antonio
- Bob Pickett, Seguin business owner
- D. P. Lyle, cardiologist and award-winning author

**Mother and son who escaped a lakeside house and camped at the motel:**

- Janie West Kothmann
- Connor West Kothmann

**Lake dwellers, present and past:**

- Jeanette West Hannasch
- Raul Guerra
- Steve and Linda Sampson
- Brian Dahl
- Linda Wallace
- Harry and Dorothy Bierstedt
- The author

# ABOUT THE AUTHOR

Nancy G. West is the author of award-winning suspense and the Aggie Mundeen mystery series.

*The Plunge*, first in a new spin-off series of Aggie Mundeen lake mysteries, was a June 2019 pick by the American Library Association's Book Club Central.

For more information about the author and her books, visit:

### Facebook:

https://www.facebook.com/authorNancyG.West/

### Website:

nancygwest.com

### Twitter:

@NancyGWest_

### Author Central:

http://tinyurl.com/authorNancyG-West

### Goodreads:

https://www.goodreads.com/author/dashboard

www.ingramcontent.com/pod-product-compliance
Lightning Source LLC
Chambersburg PA
CBHW020248150626
46552CB00020B/720